Three Hundred Years Hence

Illustrated

by Mary Griffith

Text as first published in

Camperdown; or, News from our neighbourhood:

Being sketches by the author of 'Our Neighbourhood.'

Philadelphia: Carey, Lea & Blanchard, 1836.

By Mary Griffith

(1772-1846)

THREE HUNDRED YEARS HENCE

CHAPTER I.

IT is seldom that men begin to muse and sit alone in the twilight until they arrive at the age of fifty, for until that period the cares of the world and the education of their young children engross all their thoughts. Edgar Hastings, our hero, at thirty years of age was still unmarried, but he had gone through a vast deal of excitement, and the age of musing had been anticipated by twenty years. He was left an orphan at fourteen, with a large income, and the gentleman who had the management of his estates proved faithful, so that when a person of talents and character was wanted to travel with the young man, a liberal recompense was at hand to secure his services. From the age of fourteen to twenty-one he was therefore travelling over Europe; but his education, instead of receiving a check, went on much more advantageously than if he had remained at home, and he became master of all the modern languages in the very countries where they were spoken. The last twelve months of his seven years' tour was spent in England, being stationary in London only during the sitting of Parliament.

His talents thus cultivated, and his mind enlarged by liberal travel, he returned to America well worthy the friendship and attention of those who admire and appreciate a character of his stamp. He had not therefore been back more than a year, before his society was courted by some of the best men in the country; but previous to his settling himself into *a home*, he thought it but proper to travel through his own country also. His old friend, still at his elbow, accompanied him; but at the close of the excursion, which lasted nearly two years, he was taken ill of a fever caught from an exposure near the Lakes, and died after a few days' illness.

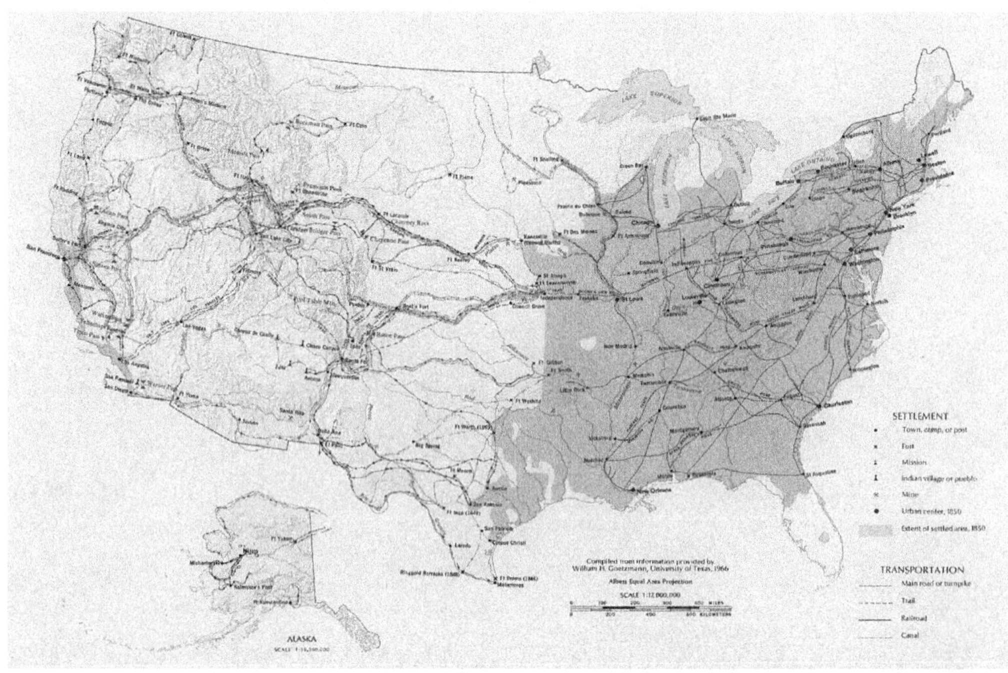

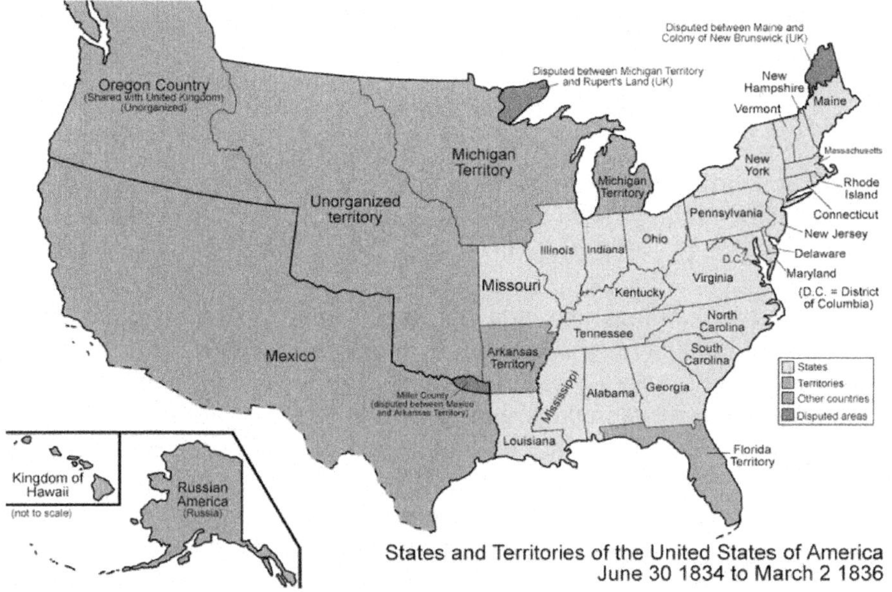

Map of the United States, 1834-1836, from Wikimedia Commons

Edgar Hastings was now entirely alone in the world, and he would have fallen into a deep melancholy, had he not engaged in politics. This occupied him incessantly; and, as his purse was ample and his heart liberally disposed, he found the demands on his time gradually increasing. He had occupations heaped upon him – for rich, disengaged, and willing, every body demanded his aid; and such were the enthusiasm and generosity of his nature, that no one applied in vain.

His first intention, on returning from his tour through his own country, was to improve an estate he had purchased in Pennsylvania, promising himself an amiable and beautiful wife to share his happiness; but politics interfered, and left him no time even for the luxury of musing in the evening. But a man can get weary of politics as well as of any other hard up-hill work; so, at the end of seven years, seeing that the young trees which he had planted were giving shade, and that the house that they were to overshadow was not yet begun, he fell to musing. He wanted something, likewise, to love and protect – so he fell to musing about that. He wished to convert a brisk stream, that fell down the side of a hill opposite to the south end of his grounds, into a waterfall – so he fell to musing about that. He wanted to make an opening through a noble piece of woods that bounded the north side, that he might catch a view of the village steeple – so he fell to musing about that. A beautiful winding river lay in front of his estate, the bank of which sloped down to the water's edge; this tranquillizing scene likewise operated on his feelings, so that politics faded away, and his mind became calm and serene. Thus it was, that at thirty years of age he had these fits of abstraction, and he became a muser.

Men of his age – sensible men – are not so easily pleased as those who are younger. He admired graceful, easy manners, and a polished mind, far before beauty or wealth; and thus fastidious, he doubted whether he should marry at all. Every now and then, too, an old bachelor feeling came over him, and he feared that when his beloved twilight found him sitting under the noble porticos which he intended to build, his wife would drag him away to some far distant route in the city; or that she would, untimely, fill the house with visiters. So, with all the dispositions in the world, he lived alone, though every fit of musing ended by finding a wife at his side, gazing on the dim and fading landscape with him.

While his house was building, he occupied a small stone farm house, at the extremity of the estate. Here he brought his valuable books and prints, well secured from damp and insects by aromatic oils; here did he draw his plans during the day, and here, under a small piazza, did he meditate in the evening, transferring his musings to the little parlour as soon as the damp evenings of autumn compelled him to sit within doors.

Adjoining his estate lived a quaker, by the name of Harley, a steady, upright man, loving his ease, as all quakers do, but having no objection to see his neighbours finer or wiser than himself. He took a fancy to our hero, and the beloved evening hour often found him sitting on the settee with Hastings, when, after enjoying together an animated conversation, he also would fall into the deep feeling which fading scenery, and the energy of such a character as his young friend's, would naturally excite in a mind so tranquil as his own.

At length, the quiet quaker spoke of his daughter, but it was not with a view to draw Edgar's attention; he mentioned her incidentally, and the young man was delighted. In a moment, his imagination depicted her as a beautiful, graceful, accomplished creature; and there could be no doubt that she was amiable and gentle; so he strolled over to his friend's house, and was regularly introduced to her. She was beautiful, and amiable, and gentle – all this he saw at a glance; but, alas! she had no accomplishment farther than that she wrote an exquisitely clear, neat hand, and was an excellent botanist and florist. But "propinquity" softened down all objections. Every time he strayed away to Pine Grove the eligibilities of the match became more apparent, and his love of grace and polish of mind seemed to be of comparatively little importance, when he listened to the breathings of the innocent quaker, who thought all of beauty was in a flower, and who infinitely preferred the perfume of a rose or a lilac, to the smell of a dozen lamps in a crowded room. Her name was Ophelia, too.

Mr. Harley, or friend Harley as he was called, was nowise rigid in his creed; for the recent lawsuits between the Orthodox and Hicksite quakers had very much weakened his attachments to the forms of quakerism. He found that the irritable portion of his society had great difficulty in keeping *hands off*, and in preserving the decorum of their order. Peaceful feelings, equable temperaments, being the foundation – the cement, which, for so many years, had bound the fraternity together, were now displaced for the anger and turbulence so often displayed by other sects of Christians.

Elias Hicks
(1748-1830)
Leader of the Hicksite Quakers

Lucretia Coffin Mott
(1793-1880)
Hicksite Quaker and Abolitionist

Litigations amongst themselves – the law – had done that which neither fine nor imprisonment, the derision nor impositions of other sects, could accomplish. The strong cement had cracked along the edge of the bulwarks, where strength was the most necessary, and the waters of discord and disunion were insinuating themselves into every opening. The superstructure was fast crumbling away, and friend Harley looked to the no very distant period when his posterity should cast off the quaker dress, and naturally follow the customs and obey the general laws which govern the whole body of Americans.

This was sensible Valentine Harley's opinion and feeling; in rules of faith he had never been inducted – are there any quakers, apart from a few of their leaders, who can define what their religious faith is? So, although he loved the forms in which he had been educated – although he wore the quaker dress, and made his son and daughter do the same – yet when Edgar Hastings left off musing in the twilight, and was seen at that hour walking slowly down the glen, with Ophelia hanging on his arm, he only heaved a sigh, and wished that the young man said *thee* and *thou*. But this sigh was far from being a painful one; he felt that when the obscure grave, which shuts out all trace of the quaker's place of rest, should close over him, his memory would live fresh and green in the heart of his daughter. Far more should he be reverenced, if he gave her gentle spirit to the strong arm, the highly gifted mind of such a man as Edgar Hastings, than if he compelled her to marry a man of their own order – to the one who was now preferring his suit, friend Hezekiah Connerthwaite, a rich, respectable, yet narrow minded and uneducated man.

That he consented to his daughter's marriage willingly, and without an inward struggle, was a thing not to be expected; but he was too manly, too virtuous, to use a mean subterfuge with his sect that he might escape the odium which falls on the parent who allows his daughter to marry out of the pale. He would not suffer his child to wed clandestinely, when in reality his heart and reason approved of her choice; when her lover's merits and claims, and her own happiness, strongly overbalanced his scruples. She might have married privately, and her father, thus rid of the blame of consenting to her apostacy, could, as usual, take his seat in their place of worship, without the fear of excommunication. But Valentine Harley scorned such duplicity and foolishness; Ophelia was therefore married under her father's roof, and received her father's blessing; and here, in this well regulated house, Edgar Hastings spent the first year of his wedded life. Here, too, his son was born; and now no longer a being without kindred or a home, he found how much happier were the feelings of a husband and father than those of a selfish, isolated being.

As he was building a spacious, elegant, and durable mansion, one that should last for many years, he went slowly to work. It was begun a year before his marriage, and it was not until his young son was three months old that he could remove his family, of which Mr. Harley now made a part, to their permanent home. The younger Harley, who had married and settled at a distance, being induced to come among them, again to take the property at Pine Grove, thus adding another link to the bond of friendship which this happy marriage had created. In the month of May the younger Harley was expected to take possession of his father's house.

It was now February. The new house was completely furnished, and every thing ready for their removal as soon as Mr. Hastings returned from New York, where he had some business of importance to transact. As it called for immediate attention, he deferred unpacking his books, or indeed taking them from the farm house, until his return. It was with great reluctance that he left his wife, who grieved as if the separation was to last for years instead of a fortnight; but he was compelled to go, so after a thousand charges to take care of her health, and imploring her father to watch over her and his little boy, he once more embraced them and tore himself away. His wife followed him with her eyes until she saw him pass their new habitation, cross over the stile and turn the angle; here he stopped to take one more look at the spot where all he loved dwelt, and seeing the group still looking towards him, he waved his handkerchief, and a few steps farther hid him from their sight.

The farm house was at the extremity of the estate, and as it lay on the road leading to the ferry, he thought he would look at the fire which had been burning in the grate all the morning. Mr. Harley said he would extinguish it in the afternoon, and lock up the house, but still he felt a curiosity to see whether all was safe. His servant, with the baggage, had preceded him, and was now waiting for him at the boat; so he hurried in, and passed from the hall to the middle room, where the books were. Here he found an old man sitting, apparently warming himself by the still glowing coals, who made an apology for the intrusion, by saying that he was very cold, and seeing a fire burning, for he had looked in at the window, he made bold to enter.

Mr. Hastings bade him sit still, but the man said he was about to cross the ferry and must hurry on, observing that he thought there would be a great thaw before morning, "and in that case," said he, pointing up to the hill, at the foot of which the house stood, "that great bank of snow will come down and crush the roof of this house." Hastings looked up and saw the dangerous position of the snow bank, and likewise apprehending a thaw, he begged the man to hurry on and tell his servant to go over with his baggage, and get all things in readiness for him on the other side, and that he would wait for the next boat, which crossed in fifteen minutes after the other. He gave the poor man a small piece of money, and after he left the house Hastings wrote a note about the snow bank to Mr. Harley, which he knew that gentleman would see, as he was to be there in the afternoon. Knowing that he should hear the steam boat bell, and feeling cold, he drew an old fashioned chair, something in the form of an easy chair, and fell into one of his old fits of musing. He thought it would not be prudent to return to his family merely to say farewell again, even if there were time, but a melancholy *would* creep over him, as if a final separation were about to take place. In vain he tried to rouse himself and shake it off; he closed his eyes, as if by doing so he could shut out thought, and it did, for in less than five minutes he was fast asleep.

CHAPTER II.

HEARING a noise, he suddenly started up. It was dusk, and having lain long in one position, he felt so stiff as to move with difficulty; on turning his head, he saw two strangers looking at him with wonder and pity. "Is the steamboat ready?" exclaimed he, still confused with his long sleep. "Has the bell rung, gentlemen? Bless me, I have overslept myself – what o'clock is it? Why, it is almost dark – I am ashamed of myself."

Finding, after one or two attempts, that he could not get up easily, the two strangers hastened forward and assisted him to rise. They led him to the door, but here the confusion of his mind seemed rather to increase than diminish, for he found himself in a strange place. To be sure, there lay the river, and the hills on the opposite shore still rose in grandeur; but that which was a wide river, now appeared to be a narrow stream; and where his beautiful estate lay, stretching far to the south, was covered by a populous city, the steeples and towers of which were still illuminated by the last rays of the sun.

"Gentlemen," said the bewildered man, "I am in a strange perplexity. I fell asleep at noon in this house, which belongs to me, and after remaining in this deep repose for six hours I awoke, and find myself utterly at a loss to comprehend where I am. Surely I am in a dream, or my senses are leaving me."

"You are not dreaming, neither is your mind wandering; a strange fate is yours," said the elder of the two young men. "When you are a little more composed we will tell you how all this has happened; meantime, you must come with me; I shall take you where you will find a home and a welcome."

"What is your name," said the astonished Hastings, "and how have I been transported hither."

"My name is Edgar Hastings," said the young man; "and I feel assured that yours is the same. If I thought you had sufficient fortitude to hear the strange events which have occurred, I would tell you at once; but you had better come with me, and during the evening you shall know all."

Hastings suffered himself to be led by the two strangers, as he felt cramped and chilly; but every step he took revived some singular train of thought. As he proceeded, he saw what appeared to be his own house, for the shape, dimensions and situation were like the one he built, and the distance and direction from his farm house was the same. What astonished him most was the trees; when he saw them last they were silver pines, chestnuts, catalpas, locusts and sycamores – now the few that remained were only oak and willow; they were of enormous size, and appeared aged.

"I must wait, I see," said poor Hastings, "for an explanation of all this; my hope is, that I am dreaming. Here lie trees newly felled, immense trees they are, and they grew on a spot where I formerly had a range of offices. I shall awake to-morrow, no doubt," said he, faintly smiling, "and find myself recompensed for this miserable dream. Pray what is your name?" – turning to the younger of the two men.

"My name is Valentine Harley, and I am related to this gentleman; our family have, at intervals, intermarried, for upwards of three hundred years."

"Valentine Harley!" exclaimed Hastings, "that is the name of my wife's father. There never was any of the name of Valentine, to my knowledge, but his; and I did not know that there was another Edgar Hastings in existence, excepting myself and my young son."

They were now in front of the house – the massive north portico had been replaced by another of different shape; the windows were altered; the vestibule, the main hall, the staircase, no longer the same – yet the general plan was familiar, and when they opened the door of a small room in the north wing, he found it exactly to correspond with what he had intended for his laboratory.

After persuading him to take some refreshments, they conducted him to his chamber, and the two young men related to the astonished Hastings what follows. We shall not stop to speak of his surprise, his sufferings, his mortal agony – nor of the interruptions which naturally took place; but the group sat up till midnight. It is needless to say that not one of the three closed his eyes the remainder of the night.

"Early this morning," began the younger Edgar Hastings – "and be not dismayed when I tell you, that instead of the 15th of February, 1835, it is now the 15th of April, 2135 – several of us stood looking at some labourers who were at work cutting a street through the adjoining hill. Our engines had succeeded in removing the trees, rocks and stones, which lay embedded in the large mounds of earth, and about ten o'clock the street, with the exception of the great mass which covered your farm house, was entirely cut through to the river. This portion of it would have been also removed, but both from papers in my possession and tradition, a stone building, containing many valuable articles, was supposed to be buried there, by the fall of the hill near which it stood.

"To extend the city, which is called Hamilton, my property, or rather, I should say, your property, was from time to time sold, till at length nothing remains in our possession but this house and a few acres of ground; the last we sold was that strip on which your farm house stands. It was with great reluctance that I parted with this portion, as I could not but consider it as your sepulchre, which in fact it has proved to be.

"When they commenced cutting through the hill the top was covered with large oaks, some of which, when sawed through, showed that they were upwards of a century old; and one in particular, which stood on the boundary line, had been designated as a landmark in all the old title deeds of two hundred years' standing.

"About three hours before you were liberated the workmen came to a solid stratum of ice, a phenomenon so extraordinary, that all the people in the vicinity gathered to the spot to talk and ponder over it. An aged man, upwards of ninety, but with his faculties unimpaired, was among the number present. He said, that in his youth his great grandfather had often spoken of a tradition respecting this hill. It was reported to have been much higher, and that a ravine, or rather a precipitous slope, a little below the road, was quite filled up by the overthrow of the hill. That the fall had been occasioned by an earthquake, and the peak of the hill, after dislodging a huge rock, had entirely covered up a stone building which contained a large treasure. He very well remembered hearing his aged relative say, that the hill was covered with immense pines and chestnuts.

"The truth of part of this story was corroborated by ancient documents in my possession, and I hastened to my library to search for some old family papers, which had been transmitted to me with great care. I soon found what I wanted, and with a map of the estate, in which, from father to son, all the alterations of time had been carefully marked down, I was able to point out the exact spot on which the old stone farm house stood. In a letter from a gentleman named Valentine Harley, which, with several from the same hand, accompanied the different maps, an account was given of the avalanche which buried the house and filled up the ravine and gap below. As the originals were likely to be destroyed by time, they had been copied in a large book, containing all the records of the family, which, from period to period, receive the attestation of the proper recording officer, so that you may look upon these documents as a faithful transcript of every thing of moment that has occurred within the last three hundred years. It was only last November that I entered an account of the sale of this very strip of land in which the stone house lay.

"Here is the first thing on record – a letter, as I observed, from the father-in-law of Edgar Hastings, my great ancestor – but I forget that it is of you he speaks. Believe me, dear sir, that most deeply do we sympathize with you; but your case is so singular, and the period in which all this suffering occurred is so very remote, that your strong sense will teach you to bear your extraordinary fate like a man. Allow me to read the letter; it is directed to James Harley, son to the above mentioned Valentine Harley.

"'Second month, 17th, 1834. My dear son – Stay where thou art, for thy presence will but aggravate our grief. I will give thee all the particulars of the dreadful calamity which has befallen us. I have not yet recovered from the shock, and thy sister is in the deepest wo; but it is proper that thou shouldst know the truth, and there is no one to tell thee but myself. On Monday the 15th, my dear son Edgar Hastings took a tender farewell of thy sister and his babe, shaking hands with me in so earnest and solemn a manner, that one prone to superstition would have said it was prophetic of evil. We saw him walk briskly along the road until the angle, which thou knowest is made by the great hill, shut him from our sight; but just before he turned the angle he cast a look towards the house wherein all his treasure lay, and seeing that we were watching his steps, he waved his handkerchief and disappeared. His intention, thou knowest, was to proceed to New York; Samuel, his faithful servant, was to accompany him, and had gone forward in the carriage with the baggage, as Edgar preferred to walk to the boat. Thy poor sister and myself stood on the old piazza waiting until the little steamboat – it was the Black Hawk – should turn the great bend and appear in sight, for it was natural, thou knowest, to linger and look at the vessel which held one so dear to us both. It was the first time that thy sister had been separated from Edgar, and she stood weeping silently, leaning on my arm, as the little steamboat shot briskly round the bend and appeared full in sight. Thou must recollect that the channel brings the boat nearly opposite the stone farm house, and even at that distance, although we could not distinguish features or person, yet we fancied we saw the waving of a handkerchief. At that instant the Black Hawk blew up, every thing went asunder, and to my affrighted soul the boat appeared to rise many feet out of the water. I cannot paint to thee our agony, or speak of the profound grief, the unextinguishable grief, of thy dear sister; she lies still in silent wo, and who is there, save her Maker, who dares to comfort her.

"'I told thee in a previous letter, written I believe on the 12th, that I apprehended a sudden thaw. I mentioned my fears to our dear Edgar, and with his usual prudence he gave orders to strengthen some of the embankments below the ravine. Among other things I thought of his valuable books and instruments, which still remained in the stone farm house, and that very afternoon I intended to have them removed to Elmwood. At the instant the dreadful explosion took place, the great snow bank, which thou recollectest lay above the house in the hollow of the hill, slid down and entirely covered the building; and, in another second, the high peak of the hill, heavily covered with large pines, fell down and buried itself in the ravine and gap below. The building and all its valuable contents lie buried deep below the immense mass of earth, but we stop not in our grief to care for it, as he who delighted in them is gone from us for ever.

"'Thy sister, thy poor sister, when the first horrible shock was over, would cling to the hope that Edgar might be spared, and it was with the greatest difficulty that I could prevent her from flying to the spot where the crowd had collected. Alas! no one lived to tell how death had overtaken them. Of the five persons engaged on board, three of their bodies have since been found; this was in dragging the water. It seems there were but few passengers, perhaps only our beloved Edgar, his poor servant Samuel, and one or two others. An old man was seen to enter the boat just as she was moving off; his body was found on the bank, and on searching his pockets a small piece of silver, a quarter of a dollar, was taken out, which I knew in a moment; it was mine only an hour before, and had three little crosses deeply indented on the rim, with a hole in the centre of the coin; I made these marks on it the day before, for a particular purpose; I could therefore identify the money at once. About an hour before Edgar left us, thinking he might want small silver, I gave him a handful, and this piece was among the number. He must have given it to the man as soon as he got on board, perhaps for charity, as the man was poor, and probably had begged of him. This at once convinced me that our dear Edgar was in the fatal boat. We have made every exertion to recover the body, but are still unsuccessful; nor can we find that of our poor faithful Samuel. The body of the horse was seen floating down the river yesterday; and the large trunk, valueless thing now, was found but this morning near the stone fence on the opposite shore.

"'There were some valuable parchments, title deeds, in a small leather valise, which our dear Edgar carried himself – but what do we care for such things now, or for the gold pieces which he also had in the same case. Alas! we think of nothing but of the loss of him, thy much valued brother. Edgar Hastings has been taken from us, and although thy poor sister is the greatest sufferer, yet *all* mourn.

"'Offer up thy prayers, my son, that God will please to spare thy sister's reason; if that can be reserved, time will soften this bitter grief, and some little comfort will remain, for she has Edgar's boy to nourish and protect. As to me, tranquil as I am compelled to be before her, I find that my chief pleasure, my happiness, is for ever gone. Edgar was superior to most men, ay, to any man living, and so excellent was he in heart, and so virtuous and upright in all his ways, that I trust his pure spirit has ascended to the Great Being who gave it.

"'Do not come to us just now, unless it be necessary to thy peace of mind; but if thou shouldst come, ask not to see thy sister, for the sight of any one, save me and her child, is most painful to her.

"'Kiss thy babe, and bid him not forget his afflicted grandfather. God bless thee and thy kind wife – Adieu, my son. VALENTINE HARLEY.'"

It need not be said that Edgar Hastings was plunged in profound grief at hearing this epistle read; his excellent father, his beloved wife, his darling child, were brought before him, fresh as when he last saw them; and now the withering thought came over him that he was to see them no more! After a few moments spent in bitter anguish, he raised his head, and motioned the young man to proceed.

"Meantime the workmen proceeded in their labours, and so great was the anxiety of all, that upwards of fifty more hands were employed to assist in removing the thick layer of ice which apparently covered the whole building. When the ice was removed, we came immediately to the crushed roof of the house, into which several of the labourers would have worked their way had we not withheld them. After placing the engines in front they soon cleared a road to the entrance, and by sundown Valentine Harley and myself stood before the doorway of the low stone farm house.

"It was not without great emotion that we came thus suddenly in view of a building which had lain under such a mass of earth for three centuries. We are both, I trust, men of strong and tender feelings, and we could not but sigh over the disastrous fate of our great ancestor, distant as was the period of his existence. We had often thought of it, for it was the story of our childhood, and every document had been religiously preserved. We stood for a few moments looking at the entrance in silence, for among other letters there were two or three, written late in life by your faithful and excellent wife – was not her name Ophelia?"

"It was, it was," said the afflicted man; "go on, and ask me no questions, for my reason is unsteady."

"In one of these letters she suggested the possibility that her beloved husband might have been buried under the ruins; that the thought had sometimes struck her; but her father believed otherwise. That within a few years an old sailor had returned to his native place, and as it was near Elmwood, he called on her to state that it was his firm belief that Mr. Hastings did not perish in the Black Hawk. His reason for this belief was, that on the way to the ship he encountered an old friend, just at that moment leaving the low stone building. 'I wanted him,' said the old sailor, 'to jump in the wagon and go with me to the wharf, but he refused, as he had business on the other side of the river. Besides, said my friend, the gentleman within, pointing to the door, has given me a quarter of a dollar to go forward and tell the captain of the Black Hawk that he cannot cross this trip. This gentleman, he said, was Mr. Hastings.'

"Another letter stated – I think it was written by the wife of James Harley, your brother-in-law – that, in addition to the above, the old sailor stated, that the ship in which he sailed had not raised anchor yet, when they heard the explosion of the Black Hawk, of which fact they became acquainted by means of a little fishing boat that came along side, and which saw her blow up. He observed to some one near, that if that was the case, an old shipmate of his had lost his life. The sailor added likewise, that he had been beating about the world for many years, but at length growing tired, and finding old age creeping on him, he determined to end his days in his native village. Among the recitals of early days was the bursting of the Black Hawk and the death of Mr. Hastings, which latter fact he contradicted, stating his reasons for believing that you were not in the boat. The idea of your being buried under the ruins, and the dread that you might have perished with hunger, so afflicted the poor Lady Ophelia that she fell into a nervous fever, of which she died."

"Say no more – tell me nothing farther," said the poor sufferer; "I can listen no longer – good night – good night – leave me alone."

The young men renewed the fire, and were about to depart, when he called them back.

"Excuse this emotion – but my son – tell me of him; did he perish?"

"No – he lived to see his great grandchildren all married: I think he was upwards of ninety when he died."

"And what relation are you to him?"

"I am the great grandson of your great grandson," said Edgar Hastings the younger; "and this young man is the eighth in descent from your brother, James Harley. We both feel respect and tenderness for you, and it shall be the business of our lives to make you forget your griefs. Be comforted, therefore, for we are your children. In the morning you shall see my wife and children. Meantime, as we have not much more to say, let us finish our account of meeting you, and then we trust you will be able to get a few hours' rest."

"Rest!" said the man who had slept three hundred years, "I think I have had enough of sleep; but proceed."

"When the thought struck us that your bones might lie under the ruins, we did not wish any common eye to see them; we therefore dismissed the workmen, and entered the door by ourselves. We came immediately into a square hall, at the end of which was the opening to what is called in all the papers the middle room; the door had crumbled away. The only light in the room proceeded from a hole which had been recently made by the removal of the ice on the roof, but it was sufficient to show the contents of the room. We saw the boxes, so often mentioned in all the letters, nine in number, and four large cases, which we supposed to be instruments. The table and four chairs were in good preservation, and on the table lay the very note which you must have written but a few minutes before the ice covered you. On walking to the other side of the room, the light fell on the large chair in which you were reclining.

"'This is the body of our great ancestor,' said Valentine Harley, 'and now that the air has been admitted it will crumble to dust. Let us have the entrance nailed up, and make arrangements for giving the bones an honourable grave.'

"'Unfortunate man,' said I; 'he must have perished with hunger – and yet his flesh does not appear to have wasted. It is no doubt the first owner of our estate, and he was buried in the fall of the ice and hill. The old sailor was right. His cap of sealskin lies at the back of his head, his gloves are on his lap, and there is the cameo on his little finger, the very one described in the paper which offered that large reward for the recovery of his body. The little valise lies at his feet – how natural – how like a living being he looks; one could almost fancy he breathes.'

"'My fancy is playing the fool with me,' said Valentine; 'he not only appears to breathe, but he moves his hand. If we stay much longer our senses will become affected, and we shall imagine that he can rise and walk.'

"We stepped back, therefore, a few paces; but you may imagine our surprise, when you opened your eyes and made an attempt to get up. At length you spoke, and we hastened to you; our humanity and pity, for one so singularly circumstanced, being stronger than our fears. You know the rest. I picked up the valise, and there it lies."

We shall draw a veil over the next two months of our hero's existence. His mind was in distress and confusion, and he refused to be comforted; but the young men devoted themselves to him, and they had their reward in seeing him at length assume a tranquil manner – yet the sad expression of his countenance never left him. His greatest pleasure – a melancholy one it was, which often made him shed tears – was to caress the youngest child; it was about the age of his own, and he fancied he saw a resemblance. In fact, he saw a strong likeness to his wife in the lady who now occupied Elmwood, and her name being Ophelia rendered the likeness more pleasing. She had been told of the strange relationship which existed between her guest and themselves; but, at our hero's request, no other human being was to know who he was, save Edgar Hastings the younger and his wife, and Valentine Harley. It was thought most prudent to keep it a secret from the wife of the latter, as her health was exceedingly delicate, and her husband feared that the strangeness of the affair might disturb her mind.

Behold our hero, then, in full health and vigour, at the ripe age of thirty-two, returning to the earth after an absence of three hundred years! Had it not been for the loss of his wife and son, and his excellent father, he surely was quite as happily circumstanced, as when, at twenty-one, he returned from Europe, unknowing and unknown. He soon made friends *then*, and but for the canker at his heart he could make friends again. He thought of nothing less than to appear before the public, or of engaging in any pursuit. His fortune, and that part of his father-in-law's which naturally would have fallen to him, was now in the possession of this remote descendent. He was willing to let it so remain, retaining only sufficient for his wants; and his amiable relation took care that his means were ample.

To divert his mind, and keep him from brooding over his sorrows, his young relative proposed that they should travel through the different states. "Surely," said he, "you must feel a desire to see what changes three hundred years have made. Are not the people altered? Do those around you talk, and dress, and live as you were accustomed to do?"

"I see a difference certainly," said Hastings, "but less than I should have imagined. But my mind has been in such confusion, and my grief has pressed so heavily on my heart, that I can observe nothing. I will travel with you, perhaps it may be of service; let us set out on the first of May. Shall we go northward first, or where?"

"I think we had better go to New York," said Edgar, "and then to Boston; we can spend the months of May, June and July very pleasantly in travelling from one watering place to another. We now go in locomotive cars, without either gas or steam."

"Is that the way you travel now?" exclaimed Hastings.

"Yes, certainly; how should we travel? Oh, I recollect, you had balloons and air cars in your time."

"We had balloons, but they were not used as carriages; now and then some adventurous man went up in one, but it was merely to amuse the people. Have you discovered the mode of navigating balloons?"

"Oh yes; we guide them as easily through the air, as you used to do horses on land."

"Do you never use horses to travel with now?"

"No, never. It is upwards of a hundred years since horses were used either for the saddle or carriage; and full two hundred years since they were used for ploughing, or other farming or domestic purposes."

"You astonish me; but in field sports, or horse racing, there you must have horses."

The young man smiled. "My dear sir," said he, "there is no such thing as field sports or horse racing now. Those brutal pastimes, thank heaven, have been entirely abandoned. In fact, you will be surprised to learn, that the races of horses, asses and mules are almost extinct. I can assure you, that they are so great a curiosity now to the rising generation, that they are carried about with wild beasts as part of the show."

"Then there is no travelling on horseback? I think that is a great loss, as the exercise was very healthy and pleasant."

"Oh, we have a much more agreeable mode of getting exercise now. Will you take a ride on the land or a sail on the water?"

"I think I should feel a reluctance in getting into one of your new fashioned cars. Do the steamboats cross at what was called the Little Ferry, where the Black Hawk went from when her boiler exploded?"

"Steamboats indeed! they have been out of use since the year 1950. But suspend your curiosity until we commence our journey; you will find many things altered for the belter."

Horse-drawn carriage on the Baltimore and Ohio Railroad
(1830-35)

The Phoenix: John Steven's first commercial Paddle Wheel Steamboat
(1809)

"One thing surprises me," said Hastings. "You wear the quaker dress; indeed, it is of
that fashion which the gravest of the sect of my time wore; but you do not use the mode
of speech – is that abolished among you?"

The young man, whom we shall in future call Edgar, laughed out. "Quaker!" said he;
"why, my dear sir, the quakers have been extinct for upwards of two centuries. My dress
is the fashion of the present moment; all the young men of my age and standing dress in
this style now. Does it appear odd to you?"

"No," said Hastings, "because this precise dress was worn by the people called Friends
or Quakers, in my day – strange that I should have to use this curious mode of speech –
my day! yes, like the wandering Jew, I seem to exist to the end of time. I see one
alteration or difference, however; you wear heavy gold buckles in your shoes, the
quakers wore strings; you have long ruffles on your hands, they had none; you wear a
cocked hat, and they wore one with a large round rim."

"But the women – did they dress as my wife does?"

"No. – Your wife wears what the old ladies before my time called a *frisk* and petticoat;
it is the fashion of the year 1780. Her hair is cropped and curled closely to her head,
with small clusters of curls in the hollow of each temple. In 1835 the hair was dressed in
the Grecian style – but you can see the fashion. You have preserved the picture of my
dear Ophelia; she sat to two of the best painters of the day, Sully and Ingham; the one
you have was painted by Ingham, and is in the gay dress of the time. The other, which
her brother had in his possession, was in a quaker dress, and was painted by Sully."

Thomas Sully
(1783-1872)

Charles Cromwell Ingham
(1796-1863)

"We have it still, and it is invaluable for the sweetness of expression and the grace of attitude. The one in your room is admirable likewise; it abounds in beauties. No one since has ever been able to paint in that style; it bears examination closely. Was he admired as an artist in your day?"

"Yes; he was a distinguished painter, but he deserved his reputation, for he bestowed immense labour on his portraits, and sent nothing unfinished from his hands."

"But portrait painting is quite out of date now; it began to decline about the year 1870. It was a strange taste, that of covering the walls with paintings, which your grandchildren had to burn up as useless lumber. Where character, beauty and grace were combined, and a good artist to embody them, it was well enough; a number of these beautiful fancy pieces are still preserved. Landscape and historical painting is on the decline also. There are no good artists now, but you had a delightful painter in your day – Leslie. His pictures are still considered as very great treasures, and they bring the very highest prices."

"How is it with sculpture? That art was beginning to improve in my day."

"Yes; and has continued to improve. We now rival the proudest days of Greece. But you must see all these things. The Academy of Fine Arts in Philadelphia will delight you; it is now the largest in the world. In reading an old work I find that in your time it was contemptible enough, for in the month of April of 1833, the Academy of Fine Arts in that city was so much in debt, as to be unable to sustain itself. It was with the greatest difficulty that the trustees could beg a sum sufficient to pay the debts. The strong appeal that was made to the public enabled them to continue it a little longer in its impoverished condition, but it seems that it crumbled to pieces, and was not resuscitated until the year 1850, at which time a taste for the art of sculpture began to appear in this country."

The First Building of the Pennsylvania Academy of the Fine Arts
(1809)

The Second Building of the Pennsylvania Academy of the Fine Arts
(1823-1845)

The Samuel M. V. Hamilton Building
(2005)

PAFA's Historic Landmark Building by Frank Furness
(1876)

On the first of May the two gentlemen commenced their tour – not in locomotive engines, nor in steamboats, but in curious vehicles that moved by some internal machinery. They were regulated every hour at the different stopping places, and could be made to move faster or slower, to suit the pleasure of those within. The roads were beautifully smooth and perfectly level; and Hastings observed that there were no dangerous passes, for a strong railing stretched along the whole extent of every elevation. How different from the roads of 1834! Then men were reckless or prodigal of life; stages were overturned, or pitched down some steep hill – rail cars bounded off the rails, or set the vehicles on fire – steamboats exploded and destroyed many lives – horses ran away and broke their riders' necks – carts, heavily laden, passed over children and animals – boats upset in squalls of wind – in short, if human ingenuity had been exerted to its fullest extent, there could not be contrivances better suited to shorten life, or render travelling more unsafe and disagreeable.

Instead of going directly to New York, as they at first contemplated, they visited every part of Pennsylvania. Railroads intersected one another in every direction; every thing was a source of amazement and amusement to Hastings. The fields were no longer cultivated by the horse or the ox, nor by small steam engines, as was projected in the nineteenth century, but by a self-moving plough, having the same machinery to propel it as that of the travelling cars. Instead of rough, unequal grounds, gullied, and with old tree stumps in some of the most valuable parts of the field, the whole was one beautiful level; and, where inclinations were unavoidable, there were suitable drains. The same power mowed the grass, raked it up, spread it out, gathered it, and brought it to the barn – the same power scattered seeds, ploughed, hoed, harrowed, cut, gathered, threshed, stored and ground the grain – and the same power distributed it to the merchants and small consumers.

"Wonderful, most wonderful," said the astonished Hastings. "I well remember this very farm; those fields, the soil of which was washed away by the precipitous fall of rain from high parts, are now all levelled smooth. The hand of time has done nothing better for the husbandman than in perfecting such operations as these. Now, every inch of ground is valuable; and this very farm, once only capable of supporting a man, his wife and five children in the mere necessaries of life, must now give to four times that number every luxury."

"Yes, you are right; and instead of requiring the assistance of four labourers, two horses and two oxen, it is all managed by four men alone! The machines have done every thing – they fill up gullies, dig out the roots of trees, plough down hills, turn water courses – in short, they have entirely superseded the use of cattle of any kind."

"But I see no fences," said Hastings; "how is this? In my day, every man's estate was enclosed by a fence or wall of some kind; now, for boundary lines I see nothing but a low hedge, and a moveable wire fence for pasturage for cows."

"Why should there be the uncouth and expensive fences, which I find by the old books were in use in 1834, when we have no horses; there is no fear of injury now from their trespassing. All our carriages move on rails, and cannot turn aside to injure a neighbouring grain field. Cows, under no pretence whatever, are allowed to roam at large; and it would be most disgraceful to the corporate bodies of city or county to allow hogs or sheep to run loose in the streets or on the road. The rich, therefore, need no enclosure but for ornament, which, as it embellishes the prospect, is always made of some pleasant looking evergreen or flowering shrub. In fact, it is now a state affair, and when a poor man is unable to enclose the land himself, it is done by money lawfully appropriated to the purpose."

"And dogs – I see no dogs," said Hastings. "In my day every farmer had one or more dogs; in little villages there were often three and four in each house; the cities were full of them, notwithstanding the dog laws – but I see none now."

"No – it is many years since dogs were domesticated; it is a rarity to see one now. Once in a while some odd, eccentric old fellow will bring a dog with him from some foreign port, but he dare not let him run loose. I presume that in your time hydrophobia was common; at least, on looking over a file of newspapers of the year 1930, called the Recorder of Self-Inflicted Miseries, I saw several accounts of that dreadful disease.

Men, women, children, animals, were frequently bitten by mad dogs in those early days. It is strange, that so useless an animal was caressed, and allowed to come near your persons, when the malady to which they were so frequently liable, and from which there was no guarding, no cure, could be imparted to human beings."

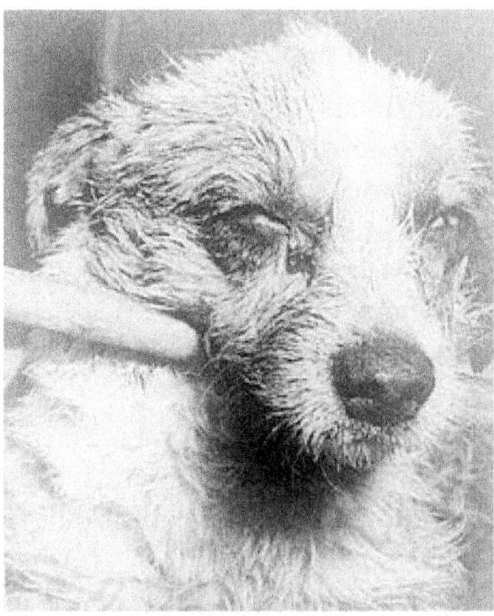
Dog with rabies virus

Louis Pasteur
(1822-1895)

"Well, what caused the final expulsion of dogs?"

"You will find the whole account in that old paper called the Recorder of Self-Inflicted Miseries; there, from time to time, all the accidents that happened to what were called steamboats, locomotive engines, stages, &c. were registered. You will see that in the year 1860, during the months of August and September, more than ten thousand dogs were seized with that horrible disease, and that upward of one hundred thousand people fell victims to it. It raged with the greatest fury in New York, Philadelphia, and Baltimore; and but for the timely destruction of every dog in the South, ten times the number of human beings would have perished. The death from hydrophobia is as disgraceful to a corporate body, as if the inhabitants had died of thirst, when good water was near them."

"This was horrible; the consternation of the people must have been very great – equal to what was felt during the cholera. Did you ever read of that terrible disease?"

"No, I do not recollect it – Oh, yes, now I remember to have read something of it – but that came in a shape that was not easy to foresee. But dogs were always known to be subject to this awful disease, and therefore encouraging their increase was shameful. Posterity had cause enough to curse the memory of their ancestors, for having entailed such a dreadful scourge upon them. The panic, it seems, was so great, that to this day children are more afraid of looking at a dog, for they are kept among wild beasts as a curiosity, than at a Bengal tiger."

"I confess I never could discover in what their usefulness consisted. They were capable of feeling a strong attachment to their master, and had a show of reason and intelligence, but it amounted to very little in its effects. It was very singular, but I used frequently to observe, that men were oftentimes more gentle and kind to their dogs than to their wives and children; and much better citizens would these children have made, if their fathers had bestowed half the pains in *breaking them in*, and in training them, that they did on their dogs. It was a very rare circumstance if a theft was prevented by the presence of a dog; when such a thing *did* occur, every paper spoke of it, and the anecdote was never forgotten. But had they been ever so useful, so necessary to man's comfort, nothing could compensate or overbalance the evil to which he was liable from this disease. Were the dogs all destroyed at once?"

"Yes; the papers say, that by the first of October there was but one dog to be seen, and the owner of that had to pay a fine of three thousand dollars, and be imprisoned for one year at hard labour. When you consider the horrible sufferings of so many people, and all to gratify a pernicious as well as foolish fondness for an animal, we cannot wonder at the severity of the punishment."

"I very well remember how frequently I was annoyed by dogs when riding along the road. A yelping cur has followed at my horse's heels for five or six minutes, cunningly keeping beyond the reach of my whip – some dogs do this all their lives. Have the shepherd's dogs perished likewise – all, did you say?"

"Yes; every dog – pointers, setters, hounds – all were exterminated; and I sincerely hope that the breed will never be encouraged again. In fact, the laws are so severe that there is no fear of it, for no man can bring them in the country without incurring a heavy fine, and in particular cases imprisonment at hard labour. We should as soon expect to see a wolf or a tiger running loose in the streets as a dog."

Every step they took excited fresh remarks from Hastings, and his mind naturally turned to the friends he had lost. How perfect would have been his happiness if it had been permitted that his wife and his father could be with him to see the improved state of the country. When he looked forward to what his life might be – unknown, alone – he regretted that he had been awakened: but his kind relative, who never left him for a moment, as soon as these melancholy reveries came over him hurried him to some new scene.

They were now in Philadelphia, the Athens of America, as it was called three centuries back. Great changes had taken place here. Very few of the public edifices had escaped the all-devouring hand of time. In fact, Hastings recognised but five – that beautiful building called originally the United States Bank, the Mint, the Asylum for the Deaf and Dumb, and the Girard College. The latter continued to flourish, notwithstanding its downfall was early predicted, in consequence of the prohibition of clergymen in the direction of its affairs. The dispute, too, about the true signification of the term "orphan" had been settled; it was at length, after a term of years, twenty, I think, decided, that the true meaning and intent of Stephen Girard, the wise founder of the institution, was to make it a charity for those children who had lost *both* parents.

The First Bank of the United States
(1797)

The Second Philadelphia Mint
(1833-1902)

Founder's Hall, Girard College
(designed 1833, completed 1847)

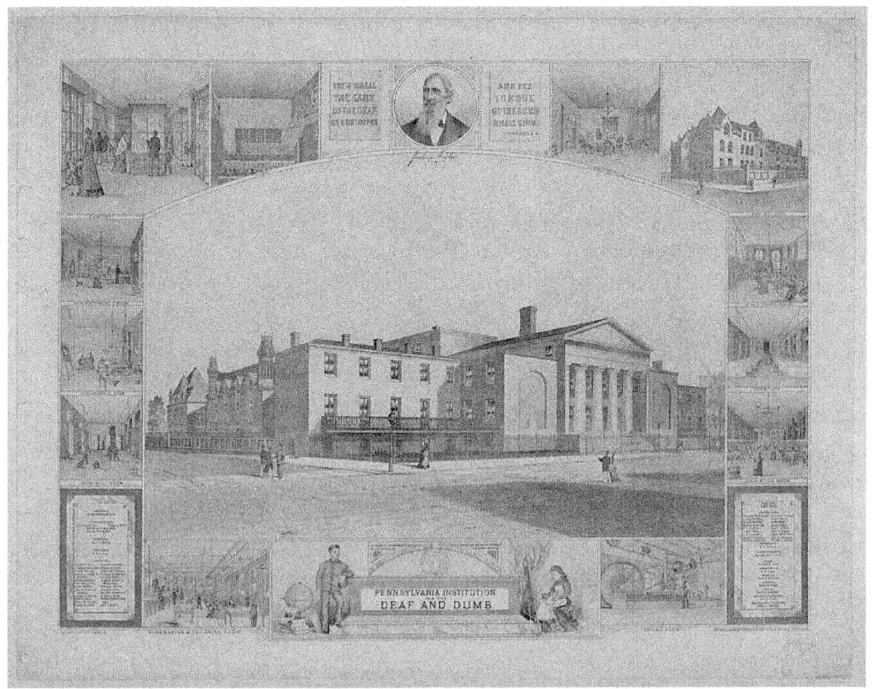

Pennsylvania Institute for the Deaf and Dumb
(1826-1893)

"I should not think," said Hastings, on hearing this from Edgar, "that any one could fancy, for a moment, that Girard meant any thing else."

"Why no, neither you nor I, nor ninety-nine out of a hundred, would decide otherwise; but it seems a question was raised, and all the books of reference were appealed to, as well as the poets. In almost every case, an *orphan* was said to be a child deprived of one or both parents; and, what is very singular, the term *orphan* occurs but once throughout the Old and New Testaments. In Lamentations it says, 'We are *orphans*, and fatherless, and our mothers are as widows.' Now, in the opinion of many, the *orphan* and *fatherless*, and those whose mothers are as widows, here mentioned, are three distinct sets of children – that is, as the lament says, *some* of us are orphans, meaning children without father and mother, *some* of us are fatherless; and the third set says, 'our mothers are as widows.' This means, that in consequence of their fathers' absence, their mothers were as desolate and helpless as if in reality they were widows by the *death* of their husbands. This text, therefore, settles nothing. Girard, like all the unlettered men of the age, by the term *orphan*, understood it to mean a child without parents."

"I very well remember," said Hastings, "that on another occasion when the term came in question, I asked every man and woman that worked on and lived near the great canal, what they meant by orphan, and they *invariably*, without a *single* exception, said it meant a child without parents."

"Well, the good sense of the trustees, at the end of the time I mentioned, decided after the manner of the multitude – for it was from this mass that their objects of charity were taken. And there is no instance on the records, of a widow begging admittance for her fatherless boys. They knew very well what being an orphan meant, but to their praise be it said, if *fatherless* children had been included in the term, there were very few who would not have struggled as long as it was in their power, before their boys should be taken to a charitable institution."

"I recollect, too," said Hastings, "that great umbrage was taken by many persons because the clergy were debarred from any interference in the management of the college. No evil, you say, has arisen from this prohibition?"

"None at all," replied Edgar. "The clergy were not offended by it; they found they had enough to do with church affairs. It has been ever since in the hands of a succession of wise, humane, and honest men. The funds have gone on increasing, and as they became more than sufficient for the purposes of the college, the overplus has been lawfully spent in improving the city."

"In the year 1835 – alas, it seems to me that but a few days ago I existed at that period – was there not an Orphan Asylum here?"

Philadelphia Orphan Asylum
(Fire, 1822)

Founder Rebecca Gratz
(1781-1869)

"Yes, my dear sir, the old books speak of a small establishment of that kind, founded by several sensible and benevolent women; but it was attended with very great personal sacrifices – for there was in that century a very singular, and, we must say, disgusting practice among all classes, to obtain money for the establishment of any charitable, benevolent, or literary institution. Both men and women – women for the most part, because men used then to shove off from themselves all that was irksome or disagreeable – women, I say, used to go from door to door, and in the most humble manner beg a few dollars from each individual. Sometimes, the Recorder of Self-Inflicted Miseries says, that men and women of coarse minds and mean education were in the habit of insulting the committee who thus turned beggars. They did not make their refusal in decent terms even, but added insult to it. In the course of time the Recorder goes on to say, men felt ashamed of all this, and their first step was to relieve women from the drudgery and disgrace of begging. After that, but it was by degrees, the different corporate bodies of each state took the matter up, and finally every state had its own humane and charitable institutions, so that there are now no longer any private ones, excepting such as men volunteer to maintain with their own money."

"Did the old Orphan Asylum of Philadelphia, begun by private individuals, merge into the one now established?"

"No," replied Edgar; "the original asylum only existed a certain number of years, for people got tired of keeping up a charity by funds gathered in this loose way. At length, another man of immense wealth died, and bequeathed all his property to the erection and support of a college for orphan girls – and this time the world was not in doubt as to the testator's meaning. From this moment a new era took place with regard to women, and we owe the improved condition of our people entirely to the improvement in the education of the female poor; blessed be the name of that man."

"Well, from time to time you must tell me the rise and progress of all these things; at present I must try and find my way in this now truly beautiful city. This is Market street, but so altered that I should scarcely know it."

"Yes, I presume that three hundred years would improve the markets likewise. But wherein is it altered?"

"In my day the market was of one story, or rather had a roof supported by brick pillars, with a neat stone pavement running the whole length of the building. Market women not only sat under each arch and outside of the pillars, but likewise in the open spaces where the streets intersected the market. Butchers and fish sellers had their appropriate stalls; and clerks of the market, as they were called, took care that no imposition was practised. Besides this, the women used to bawl through the streets, and carry their fish and vegetables on their heads."

"All that sounds very well; but our old friend, the Recorder of Self-Inflicted Miseries, mentions this very market as a detestable nuisance, and the manner of selling things through the streets shameful. Come with me, and let us see wherein this is superior to the one you describe."

The two friends entered the range above at the Schuylkill, for to that point had the famous Philadelphia market reached. The building was of two stories, built of hewn stone, and entirely fire-proof, as there was not a particle of wood-work or other ignitable matter in it. The upper story was appropriated to wooden, tin, basket, crockery, and other domestic wares, such as stockings, gloves, seeds, and garden utensils, all neatly arranged and kept perpetually clean. On the ground floor, in cool niches, under which ran a stream of cold, clear water, were all the variety of vegetables; and there, at this early season, were strawberries and green peas, all of which were raised in the neighbourhood. The finest of the strawberries were those that three centuries before went by the name, as it now did, of the *dark hautbois*, rich in flavour and delicate in perfume. Women, dressed in close caps and snow white aprons, stood or sat modestly by their baskets – not, as formerly, bawling out to the passers-by and entreating them to purchase of them, but waiting for their turn with patience and good humour. Their hair was all hidden, save a few plain braids or plaits in front, and their neck was entirely covered. Their dress was appropriate to their condition, and their bearing had both dignity and grace.

"Well, this surpasses belief," said Hastings. "Are these the descendants of that coarse, vulgar, noisy, ill dressed tribe, one half of whom appeared before their dirty baskets and crazy fixtures with tawdry finery, and the other half in sluttish, uncouth clothes, with their hair hanging about their face, or stuck up behind with a greasy horn comb? What has done all this?"

"Why, the improvement which took place in the education of women. While women were degraded as they were in your time" –

"In my time, my dear Edgar," said Hastings, quickly – "in my time! I can tell you that women were not in a degraded state then. Go back to the days of Elizabeth, if you please; but I assure you that in 1835 women enjoyed perfect equality of rights."

"Did they! then our old friend, the Recorder of Self-Inflicted Miseries, has been imposing on us – but we will discuss this theme more at our leisure. Let us ask that neat pretty young woman for some strawberries and cream."

They were ripe and delicious, and Hastings found, that however much all other things had changed, the fine perfume, the grateful flavour, the rich consistency of the fruit and cream were the same – nature never changes.

There were no unpleasant sights – no rotten vegetables or leaves, no mud, no spitting, no – in short, the whole looked like a painting, and the women all seemed as if they were dressed for the purpose of sitting for their portraits, to let other times have a peep at what was going on in a former world.

"If I am in my senses," said Hastings, "which I very much doubt, this is the most pleasing change which time has wrought; I cannot but believe that I shall wake up in the morning and find this all a dream. This is no market – it is a picture."

"We shall see," said Edgar. "Come, let us proceed to the butchers' market."

Reading Terminal Building
(1891 lithograph)

Reading Terminal Market
(2007)

So they walked on, and still the rippling stream followed them; and here no sights of blood, or stained hands, or greasy knives, or slaughter-house smells, were present. The meats were not hung up to view in the open air, as in times of old; but you had only to ask for a particular joint, and lo! a small door, two feet square, opened in the wall, and there hung the identical part.

"This gentleman is a stranger," said Edgar, to a neatly dressed man, having on a snow white apron; "show him a hind quarter of veal; we do not want to buy any, but merely to look at what you have to sell."

The little door opened, and there hung one of the fattest and finest quarters Hastings had ever seen.

"And the price," asked he.

"It is four cents a pound," replied the man. A purchaser soon came; the meat was weighed within; the man received the money, and gave a ticket with the weight written on it; the servant departed, and the two friends moved on.

"Our regulations are excellent," said Edgar; "formerly, as the old Recorder of Self-Inflicted Miseries says, the butchers weighed their meats in the most careless manner, and many a man went home with a suspicion that he was cheated of half or three quarters of a pound. Now, nothing of this kind can take place, for the clerks of the market stand at every corner. See! those men use the graduated balance; the meat is laid, basket and all, on that little table; the pressure acts on a wheel – a clicking is heard – it strikes the number of pounds and quarters, and thus the weight is ascertained. The basket you saw, all those you now see in the meat market, are of equal weight, and they are marked 1, 2, 3, 4 or more pounds, as the size may be. Do you not see how much of labour and confusion this saves. I suppose, in your day, you would have scorned to legislate on such trifling objects; but I assure you we find our account in it."

"I must confess that this simplifies things wonderfully; but the cleanliness, order and cheerfulness that are seen throughout this market – these are things worthy of legislation. I suppose all this took place gradually?"

"Yes, I presume so; but it had arrived to this point before my time; the water which flows under and through the market was conveyed there upward of a century ago. But here is beef, mutton, all kinds of meat – and this is the poultry market – all sold by weight, as it should be; and here is the fish market – see what large marble basins; each fishmonger has one of his own, so that all kinds are separate; and see how dexterously they scoop up the very fish that a customer wants."

"What is this?" said Hastings, looking through one of the arches of the fish market; "can this be the Delaware?"

"Yes," replied Edgar; "the market on which we are now, is over the Delaware. Look over this railing, we are on a wide bridge – but let us proceed to the extremity; this bridge extends to the Jersey shore, and thus connects the two large cities Philadelphia and Camden."

"In my day, it was in contemplation to build a bridge over the Delaware; but there was great opposition to it, as in that case there would be a very great delay, if not hinderance, to the free passage of ships."

New wonders sprung up at every step – vessels, light as gossamer, of curious construction, were passing and repassing under the arches of the bridge, some of three and four hundred tons burden, others for the convenience of market people, and many for the pleasure of the idle. While yet they looked, a beautiful vessel hove in sight, and in a moment she moved gracefully and swiftly under the arches, and by the time that Hastings had crossed to the other side of the bridge she was fastened to the pier.

"Is this a steamboat from Baltimore?" said Hastings. "Yet it cannot be, for I see neither steam nor smoke."

"Steamboat!" answered his companion – "don't speak so loud, the people will think you crazy. Why, steamboats have been out of date for more than two hundred years. I forget the name of the one who introduced them into our waters, but they did not continue in use more than fifty years, perhaps not so long; but so many accidents occurred through the extreme carelessness, ignorance and avarice of many who were engaged in them, that a very great prejudice existed against their use. No laws were found sufficiently strong to prevent frequent occurrences of the bursting of the boilers, notwithstanding that sometimes as many as nine or ten lives were destroyed by the explosion. That those accidents were not the consequence of using steam power – I mean a *necessary* consequence – all sensible men knew; for on this river, the Delaware, the bursting of the boiler of a steam engine was never known, nor did such dreadful accidents ever occur in Europe. But, as I was saying, after one of the most awful catastrophes that ever took place, the bursting of a boiler which scalded to death forty-one members of Congress, (on their way home,) besides upwards of thirty women and children, and nine of the crew, the people of this country began to arouse themselves, and very severe laws were enacted. Before, however, any farther loss of lives occurred, a stop was put to the use of steamboats altogether. The dreadful accident of which I spoke occurred in the year 1850, and in that eventful year a new power was brought into use, by which steamboats were laid aside for ever."

"What is the new principle, and who first brought it to light?"

"Why, a lady. The world owes this blessed invention to a female! I will take you into one of our small boats presently, where you can handle the machinery yourself. No steam, nor heat, nor animal power – but one of sufficient energy to move the largest ship."

"Condensed air, is it? – that was tried in my time."

"No, nor condensed air; that was almost as dangerous a power as steam; for the bursting of an air vessel was always destructive of life. The Recorder of Self-Inflicted Miseries mentions several instances of loss of life by the bursting of one of the air machines used by the manufacturers of mineral waters. If that lady had lived in *this* century, her memory would be honoured and cherished ; but if no memorial was erected by the English to Lady Mary Wortley Montagu, a reproach could not rest upon us for not having paid suitable honours to the American lady."

"Why, what did lady Mary Wortley Montagu do?" said Hastings; "I recollect nothing but that she wrote several volumes of very agreeable letters – Oh, yes, how could I forget – the small-pox! Yes, indeed, she did deserve to have a monument; but surely the English erected one to her memory?"

"Did they? – yes – that old defamer of women, Horace Walpole, took good care to keep the public feeling from flowing in the right channel. He made people laugh at her dirty hands and painted cheeks, but he never urged them to heap honours on her head for introducing into England the practice of innoculation for the small-pox. If this American lady deserved the thanks and gratitude of her country for thus, for ever, preventing the loss of lives from steam, and I may say, too, from shipwreck – still farther was Lady Mary Wortley Montagu entitled to distinction, for the very great benefit she bestowed on England. She saved thousands of lives, and prevented, what sometimes amounted to hideous deformity, deeply scarred faces, from being universal Yes, the benefit was incalculable and beyond price – quite equal, I think, to that which the world owes to Dr. Jenner, who introduced a new form of small-pox, or rather the small-pox pure and unadulterated by any affinitive virus. This modified the disease to such a degree, that the small-pox, in its mixed and complicated state, almost disappeared. The Recorder of Self-Inflicted Miseries states, that after a time a new variety of the small-pox made its appearance, which was called *varioloid* ; but it was quite under the control of medical skill."

Lady Mary Wortley Montagu
(1689-1762)

Edward Anthony Jenner
(1749-1823)

"Well, you live in an age so much in advance of mine, and so many facts and curious phenomena came to light during the nineteenth century, that you can tell me what the settled opinion is now respecting small-pox, kine-pox, and varioloid."

"The settled opinion now is, that they are one and the same disease. Thus – the original disease, transferable from an ulcer of the cow's udder to the broken skin of a human being, produced what is called the kine or cow-pox. This virus of the kine-pox, in its original state, was only capable of being communicated by contact, and only when the skin was broken or cut; but, when *combined* with the other poison, infected the system by means of breathing in the same atmosphere. The poison from the ulcer called cow-pox was never communicated to or by the lungs, neither was the poison which had so strong an affinity for it communicated in that way; but when the two poisons united, and met in the same system, a third poison was generated, and the *small-pox was the result.* But here we are discussing a deep subject in this busy place – what gave rise to it? – oh, steamboats, the new power now used, Lady Mary Wortley, and Dr. Jenner."

"I presume," said the attentive Hastings, "that Dr. Jenner fared no better than your American lady and Lady Mary Wortley."

"You are much mistaken," said Edgar. "Dr. Jenner was a *man*, which in your day was a very different circumstance. I verily believe if it had been a woman who brought that happy event about, although the whole world would have availed itself of the discovery, her name would scarcely be known at this day."

Hastings laughed at his friend's angry defence of women's rights, but he could not help acknowledging the truth of what was said – there was always a great unwillingness in men to admit the claims of women. But it was not a time, nor was this the place, to discuss so important a subject; he intended, however, to resume it the first leisure moment. He turned his eye to the river, and saw vessels innumerable coming and going; and on the arrival of one a little larger than that which he first saw, the crowd pressed forward to get on board as soon as she should land.

"Where is that vessel from?" said Hastings; "she looks more weather-beaten than the rest – she has been at sea."

"Yes; that is one of our Indiamen. Let us go to her, I see a friend of mine on board – he went out as supercargo."

They went on board of the Indiaman, and although it had encountered several storms, and had met with several accidents, yet the crew was all well and the cargo safe. The vessel was propelled by the same machinery – there was neither masts nor sails!

"How many months have they been on their return?" said Hastings.

"Hush!" said his friend Edgar; "do not let any one hear you. Why, this passage has been a very tedious one, and yet it has only occupied four weeks. In general twenty days are sufficient."

"Well," said Hastings, "after this I shall not be surprised at any thing. Why, in my time we considered it as a very agreeable thing if we made a voyage to England in that time. Have you many India ships?"

"Yes; the trade has been opened to the very walls of China: the number of our vessels has greatly increased. But you will be astonished to hear that the emperor of China gets his porcelain from France."

"No, I am not, now that I hear foreigners have access to that mysterious city, for I never considered the Indian china as at all equal to the French, either in texture or workmanship. But I presume I have wonders to learn about the Chinese?"

The Daoguang Emperor
(1782-1850) Qing dynasty

Empress Xiao Jing Chen
(1812-1855) Qing dynasty

"Yes, much more than you imagine. It is not more than a century since the change in their system has been effected; before that, no foreigner was allowed to enter their gates. But dissensions among themselves effected what neither external violence nor manoeuvring could do. The consequence of this intercourse with foreign nations is, that the feet of their women are allowed to grow, and they dress now in the European style. They import their fashions from France; and I see by the papers that the emperor's second son intends to pay this country a visit. They have English and French, as well as German and Spanish schools; and a great improvement in the condition of the lower classes of the Chinese has taken place; but it was first by humanizing the women that these great changes were effected. Their form of government is fast approaching that of ours, but they held out long and obstinately."

"Their climate is very much against them," observed Hastings; "mental culture must proceed slowly, where the heat is so constant and excessive."

"Yes; but, my dear sir, you must recollect that they have ice in abundance now. We carry on a great trade in that article. In fact, some of our richest men owe their wealth to the exportation of this luxury alone. Boston set the example – she first sent cargoes of ice to China; but it was not until our fast sailing vessels were invented that the thing could be accomplished."

"I should think it almost impossible to transport ice to such a distance, even were the time lessened to a month or six weeks, as it now is."

"You must recollect, that half of this difficulty of transporting ice was lessened by the knowledge that was obtained, even in your day, of saving ice. According to the

Recorder, who sneered at the times for remaining so long ignorant of the fact, ice houses could be built above ground, with the certainty that they would preserve ice. It was the expense of building those deep ice houses which prevented the poor from enjoying this luxury – nay, necessary article. Now, every landlord builds a stack of ice in the yard, and thatches it well with oat straw; and the corporation have an immense number of these stacks of ice distributed about the several wards."

"I have awakened in delightful times, my friend. Oh, that my family could have been with me when I was buried under the mountain."

Young Hastings, seeing the melancholy which was creeping over the unfortunate man, hurried him away from the wharf, and hastened to Chestnut street. Our hero looked anxiously to the right and to the left, but all was altered – all was strange. Arcades now took precedence of the ancient, inconvenient shops, there being one between every square, extending from Chestnut to Market on one side, and to Walnut on the other, intersecting the smaller streets and alleys in their way. Here alone were goods sold – no where else was there a shop seen; and what made it delightful was, that a fine stream of water ran through pipes under the centre of the pavement, bursting up every twenty feet in little jets, cooling the air, and contributing to health and cleanliness. The arcades for the grocers were as well arranged as those for different merchandize, and the fountains of water, which flowed perpetually in and under their shops, dispersed all impure smells and all decayed substances.

"All this is beautiful," said Hastings; "but where is the old Arcade – the original one?"

"Oh, I know what you mean," said Edgar; "our old Recorder states that it fell into disuse, and was then removed, solely from the circumstance that the first floor was raised from the level of the street; even in our time people dislike to mount steps when they have to go from shop to shop to purchase goods."

Arcade Hotel
Chestnut Street, west of 6th Street (1858)

William Penn
Age 22
(1644-1718)

"And what building is that? – the antiquated one, I mean, that stands in the little court. The masons are repairing it I perceive."

"That small, brick building – oh, that is the house in which William Penn lived," said Edgar. "It was very much neglected, and was suffered to go to ruin almost, till the year 1840, when a lady of great wealth purchased a number of the old houses adjoining and opened an area around it, putting the whole house in thorough repair. She collected all the relics that remained of this great man, and placed them as fixtures there, and she left ample funds for repairs, so that there is a hope that this venerable and venerated building will endure for many centuries to come."

"And what is this heap of ruins?" said Hastings, "it appears to have tumbled down through age; it was a large pile, if one may judge from the rubbish."

"Yes, it was an immense building, and was called at first the National Bank. It was built in the year 1842, during the presidency of Daniel Webster."

Second Bank of the United States
(1816-1841)
Second Bank's charter renewal was opposed
by President Andrew Jackson and supported by Daniel Webster.

Daniel Webster
(1782-1852)
Three-time unsuccessful
presidential candidate

"What," said Hastings, "was he really president of the United States? This is truly an interesting piece of news."

"News, my dear sir," said Edgar, smiling – "yes, it was news three hundred years ago, but Daniel Webster now sleeps with his fathers. He was really the chief magistrate for eight years, and excepting for the project of a national bank, which did not, however, exist long, he made an able president, and, what was very extraordinary, as the old Recorder of Self-Inflicted Miseries states, he gained the good will even of those who were violently opposed to him. He was the first president after Washington who had independence of mind enough to retain in office all those who had been favoured by his predecessor. There was not a single removal."

"But his friends – did not they complain?" said Hastings.

"It is not stated that they did; perhaps he did not promise an office to any one: at any rate the old 'Recorder' treats him respectfully. It was during his term that copyrights were placed on a more liberal footing here. An Englishman now can get his works secured to him as well as if he were a citizen of the country."

"How long is the copy right secured! it used to be, in my time," sighed poor Hastings, "only fourteen years."

"Fourteen years!" exclaimed Edgar – "you joke. Why, was not a man entitled to his own property for ever? I assure you that an author now has as much control over his own labours after a lapse of fifty years as he had at the moment he wrote it. Nay, it belongs to his family as long as they choose to keep it, just the same as if it were a house or a tract of land. I wonder what right the legislature had to meddle with property in that way. We should think a man deranged who proposed such a thing."

"But how is it when a man invents a piece of machinery? surely the term is limited then."

"Oh, yes, that is a different affair. If a man invent a new mode of printing, or of propelling boats, then a patent is secured to him for that particular invention, but it does not prevent another man from making use of the same power and improving on the machinery. But there is this benefit accruing to the original patentee, the one who makes the improvement after him is compelled to purchase a right of him. Our laws now, allow of no monopolies; that is, no monopolies of soil, or air, or water. On these three elements, one person has as good a right as another; he that makes the greatest improvements is entitled to the greatest share of public favour, and, in consequence, the arts have been brought to their present state of perfection."

"But rail-roads – surely *these* it was necessary to guarantee to a company on exclusive privilege for a term of years, even if a better one could be made."

"And I say, surely not. Why should all the people of a great nation be compelled to pass over an unsafe road, in miserably constructed cars, which made such a noise that for six hours a man had to be mute, and where there was perpetual fear of explosion from the steam engine – why should this be, when another company could give them a better road, more commodious cars, and a safer propelling power? On consulting the Recorder of Self-Inflicted Miseries, you will find that in the year 1846, the monopolies of roads, that is public roads, were broken up, and these roads came under the cognizance of the state governments, and in the year 1900 all merged under one head. There was then, and has continued ever since, a national road – the grand route from one extreme of the country to the other. Cross roads, leading from town to town and village to village, are under the control of the state governments. Here, let us get in this car which is going to Princeton; it is only an hour's ride. Well, here we are seated in nice rocking chairs, and we can talk at our ease; for the fine springs and neat workmanship make the cars run without noise, as there is but little friction, the rails of the road and the tires of the wheels being of wood. In your time this could not be the case, for as steam and manual labour were expensive, you were forced to club all together – there were, therefore, large cars that held from eight to fourteen persons; consequently, there had to be heavy iron work to keep these large machines together. Now, you perceive, the cars are made of different sizes, to accommodate either two or four persons, and they run of themselves. We have only to turn this little crank, and the machine stops. This is Bristol. It was a very small town in your day, but by connecting it to Burlington, which lies slantingly opposite, the town soon rose to its present eminence. Burlington, too, is a large city – look at the green bank yonder; it is a paradise: and look at that large tree – it is a buttonwood or sycamore; we cannot see it very distinctly; take this pocket glass. Well, you see it now at the foot of the beautiful green slope in front of the largest marble building on this bank. That tree is upwards of four hundred years old, but the house was built within the last century."

"What a change," said Hastings, as they returned to their car, – "all is altered. New Jersey, the meanest and the poorest state in the union, is now in appearance equal to the other inland states. It was in my time a mere thoroughfare. What has thus changed the whole face of nature."

"Why canals and rail roads in the first place, and rail roads now; for in a few years canals were entirely abandoned. That is, as soon as the new propelling power came into use, it was found far more economical to travel on rail roads. The track of canals through four of the principal states is no longer to be seen."

At Princeton, the first thing to be seen was the college; not the same that existed in Hastings's day, but a long, deep range of stone buildings, six in number, with work shops attached to them, after the mode so happily begun by Fellenberg. In these work shops the young men worked during leisure hours, every one learning some trade or some handicraft, by which he could earn a living if necessity required it. Large gardens lay in the rear, cultivated entirely by the labour of the students, particularly by those who were intended for clergymen, as many of this class were destined to live in the country. The college was well endowed, and the salaries of the professors were ample. It was able to maintain and educate three hundred boys – the children of the rich and the poor.

Princeton University
(1895)

45

"How do they select professors?" said Hastings; "in my day a very scandalous practice prevailed. I hope there is a change in this particular."

"Oh, I know to what you refer," said Edgar; "I read an account of it in the Recorder. It seems that when a college wanted a professor, or a president, they either wrote a letter, or sent a committee of gentlemen to the professor of another college, and told him that if he would quit the people who had with so much difficulty made up a salary for him, they would give him a hundred dollars a year more. They made it appear very plausible and profitable, and the idea of being thought of so much consequence quite unsettled his notions of right and wrong, so that, without scruple, he gave notice to his patrons that they must get another man in his place. I believe this is the true state of the case. Is it not?"

"Yes, that is the *English* of it, as we say. The funds for the support of a professor were gathered together with great difficulty, for there were very few who gave liberally and for the pure love of the advancement of learning. When by the mere force of entreaty, by appealing to the feelings, to reason, to – in short, each man's pulse was felt, and the ruling passion was consulted and made subservient to the plan of beguiling him of his money. Well, the money thus wrung from the majority, – for you must suppose that a few gave from right motives, – was appropriated to the salary of a professor, and then the question arose as to the man to be selected. They run their eye over the whole country, and, finally, the fame of some one individual induced them to consider him as a suitable candidate. This man was doing great service where he was; the college, almost gone to decay, was resuscitated by his exertions; students came from all parts on the faith of his remaining there; in fact, he had given an impulse to the whole district. What a pity to remove such a man from a place where the benefits of his labour and his energies were so great, and where his removal would produce such regrets and such a deteriorating change! But our new professor, being established in the new college, instead of going to work with the same alacrity, and with the same views, which views were to spend his life in promoting the interests of the college which he had helped to raise, now began to look '*a-head*,' as the term is, and he waited impatiently for the rise of another establishment, in the city perhaps, where every thing was more congenial to his newly awakened tastes. Thus it went on – change, change, for ever; and in the end he found himself much worse off than if he had remained in the place which first patronised him. It is certainly a man's duty to do the best he can for the advancement of his own interest, and if he can get five hundred dollars a year more in one place than in another, he has a right to do it; but the advantage of change is always problematical. The complaint is not so much against him, however, as against those who so indelicately inveigle him away."

"Yes. I can easily imagine how hurtful in its effects such a policy would be, for instance, to a merchant, although it is pernicious in every case. But here is a merchant – he has regularly inducted a clerk in all the perplexities and mysteries of his business; the young man becomes acquainted with his private affairs, and by his acuteness and industry he relieves his employer of one half of his anxieties and cares. The time is coming when he might think it proper to raise the salary of the young man, but his neighbours envy the merchant's prosperity, and they want to take advantage of the talent which has grown up under his vigilance and superintending care. 'If he does so well for a man who gives him but five hundred dollars a year, he will do as well, or better, for ten.' So they go underhandedly to work, and the young man gives the merchant notice that his neighbour has offered him a larger salary. The old Recorder is quite indignant at this mean and base mode of bettering the condition of one man or one institution at the expense of another. But was it the case also with house servants? – did the women of your day send a committee or write a letter to the servant of one of their friends, offering higher wages – for the cases are exactly similar; it is only talent of another form, but equally useful."

"Oh, no, indeed," said Hastings – "then the sex showed their superior delicacy and refinement. It was thought most disgraceful and unlady-like conduct to enveigle away the servant of a neighbour, or, in fact, of a stranger; I have heard it frequently canvassed. A servant, a clerk, a professor, or a clergyman, nine times out of ten, would be contented in his situation if offers of this kind were not forced upon him. A servant cannot feel an attachment to a mistress when she contemplates leaving her at the first offer; no tender feeling can subsist between them, and in the case of a clergyman, the consequence is very bad both to himself and his parish. In the good old times" –

"And in the good new times, if you please," said Edgar; "for I know what you are going to say. In our times there is no such thing as changing a clergyman. Why, we should as soon think of changing our father! A clergyman is selected with great care for his piety and learning – but principally for his piety; and, in consequence of there being no old clergymen out of place, he is a young man, who comes amongst us in early life, and sees our children grow up around him, he becomes acquainted with their character, and he has a paternal eye over their eternal welfare. They love and reverence him, and it is their delight to do him honour. His salary is a mere trifle perhaps, for in some country towns a clergyman does not get more than five or six hundred dollars a year, but his wants are all supplied with the most affectionate care. He receives their delightful gifts as a father receives the gifts of his children; he is sure of being amply provided for, and he takes no thought of what he is to eat or what he is to wear. He pays neither house rent, for there is always a parsonage; nor taxes; he pays neither physician nor teacher; his library is as good as the means of his congregation can afford; and there he is with a mind free from worldly solicitude, doing good to the souls of those who so abundantly supply him with worldly comforts. In your day, as the Recorder states" –

"Yes," said Hastings, "in my day, things were bad enough, for a clergyman was more imposed upon than any other professional man. He was expected to subscribe to every charity that was set on foot – to every mission that was sent out – to every church that was to be built – to every paper that related to church offices; *he had to give up all his time to his people* – literally all his time, for they expected him to visit at their houses, not when ill, or when wanting spiritual consolation, for that he would delight to do, but in the ordinary chit-chat, gossiping way, that he might hear them talk of their neighbours' backslidings, of this one who gave expensive supper parties, and of another who gave balls and went to theatres. Never was there a man from whom so much was exacted, and to whom so little was given. There were clergymen, in New York and Philadelphia, belonging to wealthy congregations, who never so much as received a plum cake for the new year's table, or a minced pie at christmas, or a basket of fruit in summer; yet he was expected to entertain company at all times. His congregation never seemed to recollect that, with his limited means, he could not lay up a cent for his children. Other salaried men could increase their means by speculation, or by a variety of methods, but a clergyman had to live on with the melancholy feelings that when he died his children must be dependent on charity. Women *did* do their best to aid their pastors, but they could not do much, and even in the way that some of them assisted their clergymen there was a want of judgment; for they took the bread out of the mouths of poor women, who would otherwise have got the money for the very articles which the rich of their congregation made and sold for the benefit of this very man. Feeling the shame and disgrace of his being obliged to subscribe to a charity, they earned among themselves, by *sewing*, a sum sufficient to constitute him a 'life member!' What a hoax upon charity! What a poor, pitiful compliment, – and at whose expense'? The twenty-five dollars thus necessary to be raised, which was to constitute their beloved pastor a life member of a charitable society, would be applied to a better purpose, if they had bought him some rare and valuable book, such as his small means could not allow him to buy."

"I am glad to hear that one so much respected by us had those sentiments," said Edgar, "for the old Recorder, even in the year 1850, speaks of the little reverence that the people felt for their clergy. Now, we vie with each other in making him comfortable; he is not looked upon as a man from whom we are to get our pennyworth, as we do from those of other professions – he is our pastor, a dear and endearing word, and we should never think of dismissing him because he had not the gift of eloquence, or because he was wanting in grace of action, or because he did not come amongst us every day to listen to our fiddle-faddle. When we want spiritual consolement, or require his services in marriage, baptism, or burial, then he is at his post, and no severity of weather withholds him from coming amongst us. In turn we call on him at some stated period, when he can be seen at his ease and enjoy the sight of our loving faces, and happy is the child who has been patted on the head by him. When he grows old we indulge him in preaching his old sermons, or in reading others that have stood the test of time, and when the infirmities of age disable him from attending to his duties, we draw him gently away and give him a competence for the remainder of his life. What we should do for our father, we do for our spiritual father."

"I am truly rejoiced at this," said Hastings, "for in my day a clergyman never felt secure of the affections of his people. If he was deficient in that external polish, which certainly is a charm in an orator, or was wanting in vehemence of action, or in enthusiasm, the way to displace him was simple and easy: dissatisfaction showed itself in every action of theirs – to sum up all, they 'held him uneasy,' and many a respectable, godly man was forced to relinquish his hold on his cure to give place to a younger and a more popular one."

"Do you send a committee to a popular clergyman, and cajole him away from his congregation, by offering him a larger salary or greater perquisites?"

"Oh no – never, never; the very question shocks me. Our professors and our clergymen are taken from the colleges and seminaries where they are educated. They are young, generally, and are the better able to adapt themselves to the feelings and capacities of their students and their congregation. Parents give up the idle desire which they had in your time, of hearing fine preaching at the expense of honour and delicacy. When a congregation became very much attached to their pastor, and he was doing good amongst them, it was cruel to break in upon their peace and happiness merely because it was in a person's power to do this. We are certainly much better pleased to have a clergyman with fine talents and a graceful exterior, but we value him more for goodness of heart and honest principles. But, however gifted he may be, we never break the tenth commandment, we never desire to take him away from our neighbour, nor even in your time do I think a clergyman would ever seek to leave his charge, unless strongly importuned."

"Pray can you tell me," said Hastings, "what has become of that vast amount of property which belonged to the — in New York?"

Third Trinity Church
(1846)

Third Trinity Church
(2010)

"Oh, it did a vast deal of good; after a time it was discovered that the trustees had the power of being more liberal with it; other churches, or rather all the Episcopal churches in the state, were assisted, and, finally, each church received a yearly sum, sufficient to maintain a clergyman. Every village, therefore, had a church and a clergyman; and in due time, from this very circumstance, the Episcopalians came to be more numerous in New York than any other sect. It is not now as it was in your time, in the year 1835; then a poor clergyman, that he might have the means to live, was compelled to travel through two, three, and sometimes four parishes: all these clubbing together to make up the sum of six hundred dollars in a year. Now this was scandalous, when that large trust had such ample means in its power to give liberally to every church in the state."

"Why, yes," said Hastings, "the true intent of accumulating wealth in churches, is to advance religion; for what other purposes are the funds created? I used to smile when I saw the amazing liberality of the trustees of this immense fund; they would, in the most freezing and pompous manner, dole out a thousand dollars to this church, and a thousand to that, making them all understand that nothing more could be done, as they were fearful, even in doing this, that they had gone beyond their charter."

"Just as if they did not know," said Edgar, "that any set of men, in any legislature, would give them full powers to expend the whole income in the cause of their own peculiar religion. Why I cannot tell how many years were suffered to elapse before they raised what was called a Bishop's Fund, and you know better than I do, how it was raised, or rather, how it commenced. And the old Recorder of Self-Inflicted Miseries, states, that the fund for the support of decayed clergymen and their families, was raised by the poor clergymen themselves. Never were people so hardly used as these ministers of the Gospel. You were an irreverend, exacting race in your day; you expected more from a preacher than from any other person to whom they gave salaries – *they* were screwed down to the last thread of the screw; people would have their pennyworth out of them. It is no wonder that you had such poor preachers in your day; why few men of liberal education, aware of all the exactions and disabilities under which the sacred cloth laboured, would ever encounter them. But, now, every village has its own pastor; and some of them are highly gifted men, commanding the attention of the most intelligent people. The little churches are filled, throughout the summer, with such of the gentry of the cities who can afford to spend a few months in the country during the warm weather. No one, however, has the indecency or the unfeelingness to covet this preacher for their own church in the city. They do not attempt to bribe him away, but leave him there, satisfied that the poor people who take such delight in administering to his wants and his comforts, should have the benefit of his piety, his learning and his example. Why, the clergymen, now, are our best horticulturists too. It is to them that we owe the great advancement in this useful art. They even taught, themselves, while at college, and now they encourage their parishioners to cultivate gardens and orchards. Every village, as well as town and city, has a large garden attached to it, in which the children of the poor are taught to work, so that to till the earth and to 'make two blades of grass grow where only one grew before,' is now the chief aim of every individual; and we owe this, principally, to our pastors. I can tell you that it is something now to be a country clergyman."

"But how were funds raised for the purchase of these garden and orchard spots!"

"Why, through the means of the *general tax*, that which, in your day, would have been called direct tax."

"Direct tax! Why my dear Edgar, such a thing could never have been tolerated in my time; people would have burnt the man in effigy for only proposing such a thing. It was once or twice attempted, indirectly, and in a very cautious way, but it would not do."

"Yes – direct tax – I knew you would be startled, for the old Recorder of Self-Inflicted Miseries states that at the close of Daniel Webster's administration something of the kind was suggested, but even then, so late as the year 1850, it was violently opposed. But a new state of things gradually paved the way for it, and now we cannot but pity the times when all the poor inhabitants of this free country were taxed so unequally. There is now, but one tax, and each man is made to pay according to the value of his property, or his business, or his labour. A land-holder, a stock-holder and the one who has houses and bonds and mortgages, pays so much per cent, on the advance of his property, and for his annual receipts – the merchant, with a fluctuating capital, pays so much on his book account of sales – the mechanic and labourer, so much on their yearly receipts, for we have no sales on credit now – that demoralizing practice has been abolished for upwards of a century."

"The merchants, then," said Hastings, "pay more than any other class of men, for there are the customhouse bonds."

"Yes," said Edgar, "I recollect reading in the Recorder of Self-Inflicted Miseries, – you must run your eye over that celebrated newspaper – that all goods imported from foreign ports had to pay duties, as it was called. But every thing now is free to come and go, and as the custom prevails all over the world, there is no hardship to any one. What a demoralizing effect that duty or tariff system produced; why honesty was but a loose term then, and did not apply to every act as it now does. The Recorder was full of the exposures that were yearly occurring, of *defrauding the revenue*, as it was called. Some of these frauds were to a large amount; and then it was considered as a crime; but when a man smuggled in hats, shoes, coats and other articles of the like nature, he was suffered to go free; such small offences were winked at as if defrauding the revenue of a dollar were not a crime *per se* as well as defrauding it of a thousand dollars – just as if murdering an infant were not as much murder as if the life had been taken from a man – just as if killing a man in private, because his enemy had paid you to do it, was not as much murder in the first degree as if the government had paid you for killing a dozen men in battle in open day – just as if" –

"Just as if what?" said the astonished Hastings, "has the time come when killing men by wholesale, in war, is accounted a crime?"

"Yes, thank Heaven," said Edgar, "that blessed time has at length arrived; it is upwards of one hundred and twenty years since men were ordered to kill one another in that barbarous manner. Why the recital of such cruel and barbarous deeds fills our young children with horror. The ancient policy of referring the disputes of nations to single combat, was far more humanizing than the referring such disputes to ten thousand men on each side; for, after all, it was 'might that made right.' Because a strong party beats a weaker one, that is not a proof that the *right* was in the strong one; yet, still, if men had no other way of settling their disputes but by spilling blood, then that plan was the most humane which only sacrificed two or one man. As to national honour! why not let the few settle it? why drag the poor sailors and soldiers to be butchered like cattle to gratify the fine feelings of a few morbidly constructed minds?"

"Oh, that my good father, Valentine Harley, could have seen this day," said Hastings. "But this bloodthirsty, savage propensity – this murdering our fellow creatures in cold blood, as it were, was cured by degrees I presume. What gave the first impulse to such a blessed change?"

Women's Peace Party
(1915)

Jane Addams
(1860-1935)
Received Nobel Peace Prize (1931)

"The old Recorder states that it was brought about by the *influence of women;* it was they who gave the first impulse. As soon as they themselves were considered as of equal importance with their husbands – as soon as they were on an equality in *money matters,* for after all, people are respected in proportion to their wealth, that moment all the barbarisms of the age disappeared. Why, in your day, a strange perverted system had taken deep root; *then,* it was the *man that was struck* by another who was disgraced in public opinion, and not the one who struck him. It was that system which fermented and promoted bloodthirstiness, and it was encouraged and fostered by men and by women both.

"But as soon as women had more power in their hands, their energies were directed another way; they became more enlightened as they rose higher in the scale, and instead of encroaching on our privileges, of which we stood in such fear, women shrunk farther and farther from all approach to men's pursuits and occupations. Instead of congregating, as they did in your time, to beg for alms to establish and sustain a charity, that they might have some independent power of their own – for this craving after distinction was almost always blended with their desire to do good – they united for the purpose of exterminating that *war seed* above mentioned – that system which fastened the *disgrace* of a blow on the one who received it. This was their first effort; they then taught their children likewise, that to kill a man in battle, or men in battle, when mere national honour was the war cry, or when we had been robbed of our money on the high seas, was a crime of the blackest die, and contrary to the divine precepts of our Saviour. They taught them to abstain from shedding human blood, *excepting in self defence* – excepting in case of invasion.

"They next taught them to reverence religion; for until bloodthirstiness was cured, how could a child reverence our Saviour's precepts? How could we recommend a wholesome, simple diet to a man who had been accustomed to riot in rich sauces and condiments? They had first to wean them from the savage propensities that they had received through the maddening influence of unreflecting men, before a reverence for holy things could be excited. Then it was that clergymen became the exalted beings in our eyes that they now are – then it was that children began to love and respect them. As soon as their fathers did their mothers the poor justice of trusting them with all their property, the children began to respect her as they ought, and then her words were the words of wisdom. It was then, and not till then, that war and duelling ceased. We are amazed at what we read. What! take away a man's life because he has robbed us of money! Hang a man because he has forged our name for a few dollars! No: go to our prisons, there you will see the murderer's fate – solitary confinement, at hard labour, for life! that is his punishment; but murders are very rare now in this country. A man stands in greater dread of solitary confinement at hard labour than he does of hanging. In fact, according to our way of thinking, now, we have no right, by the Divine law, to take that away from a human being for which we can give no equivalent. It is right to prevent a murderer from committing still farther crime; and this we do by confining him for life at hard labour, and *alone*."

"Women, you say, produced a reform in that miserable code called *the law of honour*."

"Yes, thanks be to them for it. Why, as the old Recorder states, if a man did not challenge the fellow who struck him, he was obliged to quit the army or the navy, and be for ever banished as a coward, and it was considered as disgraceful in a private citizen to receive a blow without challenging the ruffian that struck him. But the moment that women took the office in hand, that moment the thing was reversed. They entered into a compact not to receive a man into their society who had struck another, unless he made such ample apology to the injured person as to be forgiven by him; and not only that, but his restoration to favour was to be sued for by the injured party himself. A man soon became cautious how he incurred the risk."

"It often occurred to me," said Hastings, "that women had much of the means of moral reform in their power; but they always appeared to be pursuing objects tending rather to weaken than to strengthen morals. They acted with good intentions, but really wanted judgment to select the proper method of pursuing their benevolent schemes. Only look at their toiling as they did to collect funds towards educating poor young men for the ministry."

"Oh, those young men," replied Edgar, "were, no doubt, their sons or brothers, and even then they must have been working at some trade to assist their parents or some poor relation, and thus had to neglect themselves."

"No, indeed," said Hastings, "I assure you these young men were entire strangers, persons that they never saw in their lives, nor ever expected to see."

"Then, all I can say is, that the women were to be pitied for their mistaken zeal, and the men ought to have scorned such aid – but the times are altered; no man, no poor man stands in need of women's help now, as they have trades or employments that enable them to educate themselves. Only propose such a thing now, and see how it would be received; why a young man would think you intended to insult him. We pursue the plan so admirably begun in your day by the celebrated Fellenberg. When we return this way again, I will show you the work-shops attached to the college – the one we saw in Princeton."

Philipp Emanuel von Fellenberg
(1771-1844)

New York City Hall
(built 1811)

"While we are thus far on the road, suppose that we go to New York," said Hastings, "I was bound thither when that calamity befell me. I wonder if I shall see a single house remaining that I saw three hundred years ago."

Edgar laughed – "You will see but very few, I can tell you," said he, "houses, in your day, were built too slightly to stand the test of *one* century. At one time, the corporation of the city had to inspect the mortar, lest it should not be strong enough to cement the bricks! And it frequently happened that houses tumbled down, not having been built strong enough to bear their own weight. A few of the public buildings remain, but they have undergone such changes that you will hardly recognize them. The City Hall, indeed, stands in the same place, but if you approach it, in the rear, you will find that it is of marble, and not freestone as the old Recorder says it was in your time. But since the two great fires at the close of the years 1835 and 1842 the city underwent great alterations."

"Great fires; in what quarter of the city were they? They must have been disasters, indeed, to be remembered for three hundred years."

"Yes, the first destroyed nearly seven hundred houses, and about fifteen millions of property; and the second, upwards of a thousand houses, and about three millions of property; but excepting that it reduced a number of very respectable females to absolute want, the merchants, and the city itself, were greatly benefited by it. There were salutary laws enacted in consequence of it, that is, after the second fire; for instance, the streets in the burnt districts were made wider; the houses were better and stronger built; the fire engines were drawn by horses, and afterwards by a new power: firemen were not only exempt from jury and militia duty, but they had a regular salary while they served out their seven years' labour; and if any fireman lost his life, or was disabled, his family received the salary for a term of years. The old Recorder says that there was not a merchant of any enterprise who did not recover from his losses in three years."

"But what became of the poor women who lost all their property? did they lose insurance stock? for I presume the insurance companies became insolvent."

"The poor women? – oh, they remained poor – nothing in *your* day ever happened to better their condition when a calamity like that overtook *them*. Men had enough to do to pity and help themselves. Yes, their loss was in the insolvency of the insurance companies; but stock is safe enough now, for the last tremendous fire (they did not let the first make the impression it ought to have done,) roused the energies and *sense* of the people, and insurance is managed very different. Every house, now, whether of the rich or the poor man, is insured. It has to pay so much additional tax, and the corporation are the insurers. But the tax is so trifling that no one feels it a burden; our houses are almost all fire-proof since the discovery of a substance which renders wood almost proof against fire. But I have a file of the Recorder of Self-Inflicted Miseries, and you will see the regular gradation from the barbarisms of your day to the enlightened times it has been permitted you to see."

Great Fire of New York
(1835)

Croton Reservoir
(1842)

"But the water, in my day," – poor Hastings never repeated this without a sigh – "in my day the city was supplied by water from a brackish stream, but there was a plan in contemplation to bring good water to the city from the distance of forty miles."

"Where, when was that? I do not remember to have read any thing about it. – Oh, yes, there was such a scheme, and it appears to me they did attempt it, but whatever was the cause of failure I now forget; at present they have a plentiful supply by means of boring. Some of these bored wells are upwards of a thousand feet deep."

"Why the Manhattan Company made an attempt of this kind in my time, but they gave it up as hopeless after going down to the depth of six or seven hundred feet."

"Yes, I recollect; but only look at the difficulties they had to encounter. In the first place, the chisel that they bored with was not more than three or four inches wide; of course, as the hole made by this instrument could be no larger, there was no possibility of getting the chisel up if it were broken off below, neither could they break or cut it into fragments. If such an accident were to occur at the depth of six hundred feet, this bored hole would have to be abandoned. We go differently to work now; with our great engines we cut down through the earth and rock, as if it were cheese, and the wells are of four feet diameter. As they are lined throughout with an impervious cement, the overflowing water does not escape. Every house is now supplied from this never-failing source – the rich, and the poor likewise, use this water, and it is excellent. All the expense comes within the one yearly general tax: when a man builds he knows that pipes are to be conveyed through his house, and he knows also that his one tax comprehends the use of water. He pays so much per centum for water, for all the municipal arrangement, for defence of harbour, for the support of government, &c, and as there is such a wide door open, such a competition, his food and clothing do not cost half as much as they did in your day."

"You spoke of wells a thousand feet deep and four feet wide; what became of all the earth taken from them – stones I should say."

"Oh, they were used for the extension of the Battery. Do you remember, in your day, an ill constructed thing called Fort William, or Castle Garden? Well, the Battery was filled up on each side from that point, so that at present there are at least five acres of ground more attached to it than when you saw it, and as we are now levelling a part of Brooklyn heights, we intend to fill it out much farther. The Battery is a noble promenade now."

Castle Clinton
later named Castle Garden
(1808)

Aerial view of Battery Park and Financial District
(2010)

They reached New York by the slow line at two o'clock, having travelled at the rate of thirty miles an hour; and after walking up Broadway to amuse themselves with looking at the improvements that had taken place since Hastings last saw it – three hundred years previous – they stopped at the Astor Hotel. This venerable building, the City Hall, the Public Mart, the St. Paul's Church, and a stone house at the lower end of the street, built by governor Jay, were all that had stood the test of ages. The St. Paul was a fine old church, but the steeple had been taken down and a dome substituted, as was the fashion of all the churches in the city – the burial yards of all were gone – houses were built on them: – vaults, tombs, graves, monuments – what had become of them?

St. Paul's Chapel, Astor House, U.S. Post Office

The Astor Hotel, a noble building, of simple and chaste architecture, stood just as firm, and looked just as well, as it did when Hastings saw it. Why should it not? stone is stone, and three hundred years more would pass over it without impairing it. This shows the advantage of stone over brick. Mr. Astor built for posterity, and he has thus perpetuated his name. He was very near living as long as this building; the planning and completing of it seemed to renovate him, for his life was extended to his ninety-ninth year. This building proves him to have been a man of fine taste and excellent judgment, for it still continues to be admired.

"But how is this?" said Hastings, "I see no houses but this one built by Mr. Astor that are higher than three stories; it is the case throughout the city, stores and all."

"Since the two great fires of 1835 and 1842, the corporation forbid the building of any house or store above a certain height. Those tremendous fires, as I observed, brought people to their senses, and they now see the folly of it.

"The ceilings are not so high as formerly; more regard is shown to comfort. Why the old Recorder of Self-Inflicted Miseries states, that men were so indifferent about the conveniences and comforts of life, that they would sometimes raise the ceilings to the great height of fourteen and fifteen feet! Nay, that they did so in despite of their wives' health, never considering how hard it bore on the lungs of those who were affected with asthma or other visceral complaints. Heavens and earth! how little the ease and pleasure of women were consulted in your day."

"Yes, that appears all very true," said Hastings, "but you must likewise recollect that these very women were quite as eager as their husbands to live in houses having such high flights of stairs."

"Poor things," exclaimed Edgar, "to think of their being trained to like and desire a thing that bore so hard on them. Only consider what a loss of time and breath it must be to go up and down forty or fifty times a day, for your nurseries were, it seems, generally in the third story. We love our wives too well now to pitch our houses so high up in the air. The Philadelphians had far more humanity, more consideration; they always built a range of rooms in the rear of the main building, and this was a great saving of time and health."

"Where, at length, did they build the custom house?" said Hastings; "I think there was a difficulty in choosing a suitable spot for it."

"Oh, I recollect," said Edgar. "Why they did at length decide, and one was built in Pine street; but that has crumbled away long since. You know that we have no necessity for a custom house now, as all foreign goods come free of duty. This direct tax includes all the expenses of the general and state governments, and it operates so beautifully that the rich man now bears his full proportion towards the support of the whole as the poor man does. This was not the case in your day. Only think how unequally it bore on the labourer who had to buy foreign articles, such as tea, and sugar, and coffee, for a wife and six or eight children, and to do all this with his wealth, which was the labour of his hands. The rich man did not contribute the thousandth part of his proportion towards paying for foreign goods, nor was he taxed according to his revenue for the support of government. The direct tax includes the poor man's wealth, which is his labour, and the rich man's wealth, which is his property."

Alexander Hamilton U.S. Custom House
(built 1901-1907)

Merchants Exchange Building
55 Wall Street
(built 1836-1841)

"But have the merchants no mart – no exchange? According to the map you showed me of the two great fires, the first exchange was burnt."

"Yes, the merchants have a noble exchange. Did you not see that immense building on State street, surrounded by an area? After the first great fire they purchased – that is, a company purchased – the whole block that included State street in front, Pearl street in the rear, and Whitehall street at the lower end. All mercantile business is transacted there, the principal post office and the exchange are there now; the whole go under the general name of Mart – the City Mart."

"Is it not inconvenient to have the post office so far from the centre of business? – it was a vexed question in my day," said Hastings.

"You must recollect that even then, central as the post office was, there were many sub-post offices. If men in your day were regardless of the many unnecessary steps that their wives were obliged to take, they were very careful of sparing themselves. We adopt the plan now of having two sets of post men or letter carriers; one set pass through the streets at a certain hour to receive letters, their coming being announced by the chiming of a few bells at their cars, and the other set delivering letters. They both ride in cars, for now that no letter, far or near, pays more than two cents postage – which money is to pay the letter carriers themselves – the number of letters is so great that cars are really necessary. All the expense of the post office department is defrayed from the income or revenue of the direct tax – and hence the man of business pays his just proportion too. It was a wise thing, therefore, to establish all the mercantile offices near the Battery; they knew that the time was coming when New York and Brooklyn would be as one city."

"One city!" exclaimed Hastings; "how can that be? If connected by bridges, how can the ships pass up the East river?"

"You forget that our vessels have no masts; they pass under the bridges here as they do in the Delaware."

"Oh, true, I had forgotten; but my head is so confused with all the wonders that I see and hear, that you must excuse my mistakes. The old theatre stood there, but it has disappeared, I suppose. It was called the Park Theatre. How are the play houses conducted now? is there only one or two good actors now among a whole company?"

Park Theatre
Manhattan, New York
(1798-1848)

Broadway Theatre District
New York
(2013)

"Well, that question really does amuse me. I dare say that the people of your day were as much astonished at reading the accounts handed down to them of the fight of gladiators before an audience, as we are at your setting out evening after evening to hear the great poets travestied. If we could be transported back to your time, how disgusted we should be to spend four hours in listening to rant and ignorance. All our actors now, are men and women of education, such as the Placides, the Wallacks, the Kembles, the Keans, of your day. I assure you, we would not put up with inferior talent in our cities. It is a rich treat now to listen to one of Shakspeare's plays, for every man and woman is perfect in the part. The whole theatrical corps is held in as much esteem, and make a part of our society, as those of any other profession do. The worthless and the dissolute are more scrupulously rejected by that body than they are from the body of lawyers or doctors; in fact it is no more extraordinary now, than it was in your day to see a worthless lawyer, or merchant, or physician, and to see him tolerated in society too, if he happen to be rich. But there is no set of people more worthy of our friendship and esteem than the players. A great change, to be sure, took place in their character, as soon as they had reaped the benefit of a college education. I presume you know that there is a college now for the education of public actors?"

"Is it possible?" said Hastings; "then I can easily imagine the improvements you speak of; for with the exception of the few – the stars, as they were called – there was but little education among them."

"Here it is that elocution is taught, and here all public speakers take lessons," said Edgar; "you may readily imagine what an effect such an institution would have on those who intended to become actors. In your day, out of the whole theatrical corps of one city, not more than six or seven, perhaps, could tell the meaning of the *words* they used in speaking, to say nothing of the *sense* of the author. There is no more prejudice now against play-acting than there is against farming. The old Recorder states, that, before our revolution, the farmers were of a more inferior race, and went as little into polite society as the mechanics did. Even so far back as your time a farmer was something of a gentleman, and why an actor should not be a gentleman is to us incomprehensible. One of the principal causes of this change of personal feeling towards actors has arisen from our having expunged all the low and indelicate passages from the early plays. Shakspeare wrote as the times then were, but his works did not depend on a few coarse and vulgar passages for their popularity and immortality; they could bear to be taken out, as you will perceive, for the space they occupied is not now known; the adjoining sentence closed over them, as it were, and they are forgotten. There were but few erasures to be made in the writings of Sir Walter Scott; the times were beginning to loathe coarse and indelicate allusions in your day, and, indeed, we may thank the other sex for this great improvement. They never disgraced their pages with sentences and expressions which would excite a blush. Look at the purity of such writers as Miss Burney, Mrs. Radcliffe, Miss Edgeworth, Miss Austin, Madame Cotton, and others of their day in Europe, – it is to woman's influence that we owe so much. See what is done by them now; why they have fairly routed and scouted out that vile, disgraceful, barbarous practice which was even prevalent in your time – that of beating and bruising the tender flesh of their children."

"I am truly rejoiced at that," said Hastings, "but I hope they extended their influence to the schools likewise – I mean the common schools; for, in my day in the grammar school of a college, a man who should bruise a child's flesh by beating or whipping him would have been kicked out of society."

"Why, I thought that boys were whipped in the grammar schools also. In the year 1836, it appears to me, that I remember to have read of the dismissal of some professor for injuring one of the boys by flogging him severely."

"I do not recollect it; but you say 1836 – alas! I was unconscious then. It was the remains of barbarism; how a teacher could get roused to such height of passion as to make him desire to bruise a child's flesh, I cannot conceive – when the only crime of the poor little sufferer was either an unwillingness or an inability to recite his lessons. I can imagine that a man, when drunk, might bruise a child's flesh in such a shocking manner as that the blood would settle under the skin, because liquor always brutalizes. Is drunkenness as prevalent now as formerly?"

"Oh no, none but the lowest of the people drink to excess now, and they have to get drunk on cider and wine, for spirituous liquors have been prohibited by law for upwards of two hundred years. A law was passed in the year 1901, granting a divorce to any woman whose husband was proved to be a drunkard. This had a good effect, for a drunkard knew that if he was abandoned by his wife he must perish; so it actually reclaimed many drunkards at the time, and had a salutary effect afterwards. Besides this punishment, if a single man, or a bachelor, as he is called, was found drunk three times, he was put in the workhouse and obliged to have his head shaved, and to work at some trade. It is a very rare thing to see a drunkard now. But what are you looking for?"

Spirituous Liquors

A Cigar Box

"I thought I might see a cigar box about – not that I ever smoke" –

"A what? – a cigar? Oh yes, I know – little things made of tobacco leaves; but you have to learn that there is not a tobacco plantation in the world now. That is one of the most extraordinary parts of your history: that well educated men could keep a pungent and bitter mass of leaves in their mouth for the pleasure of seeing a stream of yellow water running out of it, is the most incomprehensible mystery to me; and then, to push the dust of these leaves up their nostrils, which I find by the old Recorder that they did, for the mere pleasure of hearing the noise that was made by their noses! The old Recorder called their pocket handkerchiefs flags of abomination."

Hastings thought it was not worth while to convince the young man that the disgusting practice was not adopted for such purposes as he mentioned. In fact his melancholy had greatly increased since their arrival in this city, and he determined to beg his young friend to return the next day to their home, and to remain quiet for another year, to see if time could reconcile him to his strange fate. He took pleasure in rambling through the city hall, and the park, which remained still of the same shape, and he was pleased likewise to see that many of the streets at right angles with Broadway were more than twice the width that they were in 1835. For instance, all the streets from Wall street up to the Park were as wide as Broadway, and they were opened on the other side quite down to the Hudson.

"Yes," said Edgar, "it was the great fire of 1842 which made this salutary change; but here is a neat building – you had nothing of this kind in your time. This is a house where the daughters of the poor are taught to sew and cut out wearing apparel. I suppose you know there are no men tailors now."

The Philadelphia School of Design for Women was founded in 1848, and located in the Edwin Forrest House from 1880-1959. It became Moore College of Art & Design in 1989.

Sarah Worthington Peter
PSDW Founder
(1800-1877)

The New York School of Design for Women was founded in 1852 and became the Women's Art School of the The Cooper Union by 1859.

Mary Morris Hamilton
NYSDW Founder
(1818-1877)

"What, do women take measure?"

"Oh no, men are the measurers, but women cut out and sew. It is of great advantage to poor women that they can cut out and make their husbands' and children's clothes. The old Recorder states that women – poor women – in the year 1836, were scarcely able to cut out their own clothes. But just about that date, a lady of this city suggested the plan of establishing an institution of this kind, and it was adopted. Some benevolent men built the house and left ample funds for the maintenance of a certain number of poor girls, with a good salary for those who superintend it. And here is another house: this is for the education of those girls whose parents have seen better days. Here they are taught accounts and book-keeping – which, however, in our day is not so complicated as it was, for there is no credit given for any thing. In short these girls are instructed in all that relates to the disposal of money; our women now comprehend what is meant by stocks, and dividends, and loans, and tracts, and bonds, and mortgages."

"Do women still get the third of their husband's estate after their husband's death?"

"Their thirds? I don't know what you mean – Oh, I recollect; yes, in your day it was the practice to curtail a woman's income after her husband's death. A man never then considered a woman as equal to himself; but, while he lived, he let her enjoy the whole of his income equally with himself, because he could not do otherwise and enjoy his money; but when he died, or rather, when about making his will, he found out that she was but a poor creature after all, and that a very little of what he had to leave would suffice for her. Nay, the old Recorder says that there have been rich men who ordered the very house in which they lived, and which had been built for their wives' comfort, during their life time, to be sold, and who thus compelled their wives to live in mean, pitiful houses, or go to lodgings."

"Yes," said Hastings, – quite ashamed of his own times, – "but then you know the husband was fearful that his wife would marry again, and all their property would go to strangers."

"Well, why should not women have the same privileges as men? Do you not think that a woman had the same fears? A man married again and gave his money to strangers – did he not? The fact is, we consider that a woman has the same feelings as we have ourselves – a thing you never once thought of – and now the property that is made during marriage is as much the woman's as the man's; they are partners in health and in sickness, in joy and in sorrow – they enjoy every thing in common while they live together, and why a woman, merely on account of her being more helpless, should be cut off from affluence because she survives her husband, is more than we of this century can tell. Why should not children wait for the property till after her death, as they would for their father's death? It was a relic of barbarism, but it has passed away with wars and bloodshed. We educate our women now, and they are as capable of taking care of property as we are ourselves. They are our trustees, far better than the trustees you had amongst you in your day – they seldom could find it in their hearts to allow a widow even her poor income. I suppose they thought that a creature so pitifully used by her husband was not worth bestowing their honesty upon."

"But the women in my day," said Hastings, "seemed to approve of this treatment; in fact, I have known many very sensible women who thought it right that a man should not leave his wife the whole of his income after his death. But they were beginning to have their eyes opened, for I recollect that the subject was being discussed in 1835."

"Yes, you can train a mind to acquiesce in any absurd doctrine, and the truth is, that as women were then educated, they were, for the most part, unfit to have the command of a large estate. But I cannot find that the children were eventually benefited by it; for young men and women, coming into possession of their father's estate at the early age of twenty-one, possessed no more business talent than their mother; nor had they even as much prudence and judgment in the management of money matters, as she had. Men seldom thought of this, but generally directed their executors to divide the property among the children as soon as they became of age – utterly regardless of the injustice they were doing their wives, and of the oath which they took when they married – that is, if they married according to the forms of the Episcopal church. In that service, a man binds himself by a solemn oath 'to endow his wife with *all* his worldly goods.' If he swears to endow her with all, how can he in safety to his soul, *will* these worldly goods away from her. We consider the practice of depriving a woman of the right to the whole of her husband's property after his death, as a monstrous act of injustice, and the laws are now peremptory on this subject."

"I am certain you are right," said Hastings, "and you have improved more rapidly in this particular, during a period of three hundred years, than was done by my ancestors in two thousand years before. I can understand now, how it happens, that children have the same respect for their mother, that they only felt for their father in my time. The custom, or laws, being altogether in favour of equality of rights between the parents, the children do not repine when they find that they stand in the same relation of dependence to their mother, that they did to their father; and why this should not be, is incomprehensible to me now, but I never reflected on it before."

"Yes, there are fewer estates squandered away in consequence of this, and society is all the better for it. Then to this is added the great improvement in the business education of women. All the retail and detail of mercantile operations are conducted by them. You had some notion of this in your time; for, in Philadelphia, although women were generally only employed to make sales behind the counter, yet some were now and then seen at the head of the establishment. Before our separation from Great Britain, the business of farming was also at a low ebb, and a farmer was but a mean person in public estimation. He ranks now amongst the highest of our business men; and in fact, he is equal to any man whether in business or not, and this is the case with female merchants. Even in 1836, a woman who undertook the business of a retail shop, managing the whole concern herself, although greatly respected, she never took her rank amongst the first classes of society. This arose, first, from want of education, and, secondly, from her having lived amongst an inferior set of people. But when women were trained to the comprehension of mercantile operations, and were taught how to dispose of money, their whole character underwent a change, and with this accession of business talent, came the respect from men for those who had a capacity for the conducting of business affairs. Only think what an advantage this is to our children; why our mothers and wives are the first teachers, they give us sound views from the very commencement, and our clerkship begins from the time we can comprehend the distinction of right and wrong."

"Did not our infant schools give a great impulse to this improvement in the condition of women, and to the improvement in morals, and were not women mainly instrumental in fostering these schools?"

"Yes, that they were; it was chiefly through the influence of their pen and active benevolence, that the scheme arrived at perfection. In these infant schools a child was early taught the mystery of its relation to society; all its good dispositions and propensities were encouraged and developed, and its vicious ones were repressed. The world owes much to the blessed influence of infant schools, and the lower orders were the first to be humanized by them. But I need not dwell on this particular. I shall only point to the improvement in the morals of our people at this day, to convince you that it is owing altogether to the benign influence of women. As soon as they took their rank as an equal to man, equal as to property I mean, for they had no other right to *desire*; there was no longer any struggle, it became their ambition to show how long the world had been benighted by thus keeping them in a degraded state. I say degraded state, for surely it argued in them imbecility or incapacity of some kind, and to great extent, too, when a man appointed executors and trustees to his estate whilst his wife was living. It showed one of three things – that he never considered her as having equal rights with himself; or, that he thought her incompetent to take charge of his property – or, that the customs and laws of the land had so warped his judgment, that he only did as he saw others do, without considering whether these laws and customs were right or wrong. But if you only look back you will perceive, that in every benevolent scheme, in every plan for meliorating the condition of the poor, and improving their morals, it was women's influence that promoted and fostered it. It is to that healthy influence, that we owe our present prosperity and happiness – and it is an influence which I hope may forever continue."

It was not to such a man as Hastings that Edgar need have spoken so earnestly; he only wanted to have a subject fairly before him to comprehend it in all its bearings. He rejoiced that women were now equal to men in all that they ever considered as their rights; and he rejoiced likewise that the proper distinction was rigidly observed between the sexes – that as men no longer encroached on their rights, they, in return, kept within the limits assigned them by the Creator. As a man and a christian, he was glad that this change had taken place; and it was a melancholy satisfaction to feel that with these views, if it had been permitted him to continue with his wife, he should have put her on an equality with himself.

The moment his wife and child appeared to his mental vision, he became indifferent to what was passing around him; Edgar, perceiving that he was buried in his own thoughts, proposed that they should return home immediately, and they accordingly passed down Broadway to the Battery, from which place they intended to take a boat. They reached the wharf – a ship had just arrived from the Cape of Good Hope, with a fine cargo. The captain and crew of which were black.

– "That is true," said Hastings, "I have seen very few negroes; what has become of them. The question of slavery was a very painful one in my time, and much of evil was apprehended in consequence of a premature attempt to hasten their emancipation. I dread to hear how it eventuated."

"You have nothing to fear on that score," said Edgar, "for the whole thing was arranged most satisfactorily to all parties. The government was rich in resources, and rich in land; they sold the land, and with the money thus obtained, and a certain portion of the surplus revenue in the course of ten years, they not only indemnified the slaveholders for their loss of property, but actually transplanted the whole of the negro population to Liberia, and to other healthy colonies. The southern planters soon found that their lands could be as easily cultivated by the labour of white men, as by the negroes."

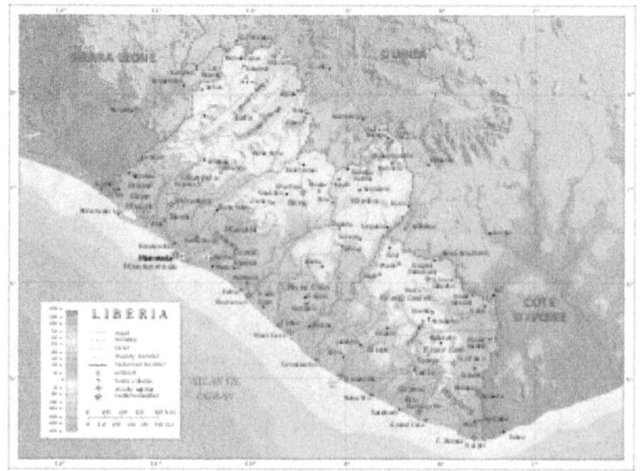
Liberia
(1821-1822)

John Randolph, co-founder of the American Colonization Society (1773-1833)

"But a great number remained, I presume, for it would not have been humane to force those to go who preferred to stay."

"All that chose to settle in this country were at liberty to do so, and their rights and privileges were respected; but in the course of twenty or thirty years, their descendants gradually went over to their own people, who by this time, had firmly established themselves."

"Did those that remained, ever intermarry with the white population, and were they ever admitted into society?"

"As soon as they became free, as soon as their bodies were unshackled, their minds became enlightened, and as their education advanced, they learned to appreciate themselves properly. They saw no advantage in intermarrying with the whites; on the contrary, they learned, by close investigation, that the negro race becomes extinct in the fourth remove, when marriages took place between the two colours. It seemed to be their pride to keep themselves a distinct people, and to show the world that their organization allowed of the highest grade of mental culture. They seemed utterly indifferent likewise about mixing in the society of white men, for their object and sole aim was to become independent. Many of their descendants left the United States with handsome fortunes. You could not insult a black man more highly than to talk of their intermarrying with the whites – they scorn it much more than the whites did in your time."

"How do they treat the white people that trade with them in their own country?"

"How? why as Christians – to their praise be it said, they never retaliated. The few excesses they committed whilst they were degraded by slavery, was entirely owing to a misdirection of their energies; but the moment the white man gave up his right over them, that moment all malignant and hostile feelings disappeared. The name of negro is no longer a term of reproach, he is proud of it; and he smiles when he reads in the history of their servitude, how indignant the blacks were at being called by that title. They are a prosperous and happy people, respected by all nations, for their trade extends over the whole world. They would never have arrived at their present happy condition if they had sought to obtain their freedom by force; but by waiting a few years – for the best men of their colour saw that the spirit of the times indicated that their day of freedom was near – they were released from bondage with the aid and good wishes of the whole country. It showed their strong good sense in waiting for the turn of the tide in their favour; it proved that they had forethought, and deserved our sympathies."

"I am glad of all this," said Hastings – "and the Indians – what has become of them, are they still a distinct people?"

"I am sorry you ask that question, – for it is one on which I do not like to converse – but

'The Indians have departed – gone is their hunting ground,
And the twanging of their bow-string is a forgotten sound.
Where dwelleth yesterday – and where is echo's cell?
Where hath the rainbow vanished – there doth the Indian dwell!'

"When our own minds were sufficiently enlightened, when our hearts were sufficiently inspired by the humane principles of the Christian religion, we emancipated the blacks. What demon closed up the springs of tender mercy when Indian rights were in question I know not? – but I must not speak of it!"

The Trail of Tears
(1831-1839)

Andrew Jackson
President (1829-1837)

They now proceeded homewards, and in three hours – for they travelled slowly, that they might the better converse, – they came in sight of the low, stone farm-house, in which poor Hastings had taken his nap of three hundred years. They alighted from the car, and as he wished to indulge himself in taking one more look at the interior – for the building was soon to be removed – his young relative left him to apprize his family of their arrival. After casting a glance at Edgar, he entered the house, and seating himself mechanically in the old arm chair, he leaned his head back in mournful reverie. Thoughts innumerable, and of every variety chased each other through his troubled brain; his early youth, his political career, his wife and child, all that they had ever been to him, his excellent father, Valentine Harley, and all their tender relationship, mingled confusedly with the events that had occurred since his long sleep – copy-rights – mad dogs – bursting of steam boilers – the two great fires in New-York – direct tax – no duties – post-offices – the improved condition of clergymen – no more wars – no bruising of children's flesh – women's rights – Astor's hotel – New-York Mart in State-street – Negro emancipation – all passed in rapid review, whilst his perplexities to know what became of the Indians were mixed with the rest, and ran through the whole scene. At the same time that all this was galloping through his feverish brain, he caught a glance of his young relative, and in his troubled imagination, it appeared that it was not the Edgar Hastings who had of late been his kind companion, but his own son. He was conscious that this was only a trick of the fancy, and arose from his looking so earnestly at the young man as he left him at the door of the house; but it was a pleasant fancy, and he indulged in it, till a sudden crash or noise of some kind jarred the windows and aroused him. He was sensible that footsteps approached, and he concluded it was his young friend who had returned to conduct him home.

"Edgar – Edgar Hastings – my son is it thou – didst thou not hear the cannon of the Black Hawk – hast thou been sleeping?"

"Amazement! Was that the voice of his father – was this the good Valentine Harley that now assisted him to rise – and who were those approaching him – was it his darling wife, and was that smiling boy his own son, his little Edgar!"

"You have been asleep, I find, my dear husband," said the gentle Ophelia, "and a happy sleep it has been for me, for us all. See, here is a letter which makes it unnecessary for you to leave home."

"And is this reality? – do I indeed hold thee to my heart once more, my Ophelia – oh, my father, what a dream!"

THE END

CPSIA information can be obtained
at www.ICGtesting.com
Printed in the USA
LVOW04s0139130716
496107LV00009B/77/P